The Other Side
of
the Mirror

Eugene L. Weems
Timothy R. Richardson

Universal Publishing LLC

THE OTHER SIDE OF THE MIRROR

For information, go to: http://www.UniversalPublishingLLC.com

May be purchased for educational, business, or sales promotional use. For information, please write: Universal Publishing, LLC
Special Markets Department
P.O. Box 99491
Emeryville, California 94662

Cover Design: Stephani Richardson
Editor: Terri Harper
http://www.terristranscripts.net

ISBN: 978-0-9840456-0-0

Library of Congress Cataloguing-in-Publication Data: 2011939313

Universal Publishing, LLC

Printed in the United States of America

This book is dedicated to our mothers,
Aldine Weems and
Yvonne Aubrey-McWoodson,
without whom this book would
not have been possible.

ACKNOWLEDGEMENTS

Annie Montgomery, Aldine Weems, Larae Weems, Henry Ridley, Sr., Henry Ridley, Jr., Madine Montgomery, Larry Bolden, James Weems, Larry Weems, Bee Johnson, Nicole Hall, Robert Swain, Timothy Blackburn, Tiana & Tiara Blackburn, and Sophia Lim. You are all dearly remembered.

As the final credits roll for *United We Stand*, it's time for me to express my deepest appreciation and warmest thanks to the most important person in my life, **Mrs. Betty Sue Ridley**, who is my loyal aunty, the other queen next to my grandmother, Mrs. Aldine Weems, who remains at the top of the pedestal of my realm. The woman who helped raise such a handsome, respectful, successful man. How can I ever show or express my gratitude to God for being blessed with you both? Such words of appreciation seem not to exist in this world. Your love for me has been unconditional, not just by word of mouth but by your actions. You are everything in a woman that many other women only wish they could be, and that every man wishes they could have in their lives. I love you, Tee-Tee, beyond eternity.

My love and respect go out to the following people: Michael Payton, Kisha Gray, Antralisa Shavette Alexander, Elizabeth Hall, Andrea Calloway, Alicia *Black Diamond* Griffin, Gwendolyn James, KeyonJane Whittle, Thelma Adams, Janet A. Berger, Nate J.B. Brown, Marquichea Burns, Theodore *Ted* Cole, Sheila Devereaux, Chi Ali Griffith, Heather Hall, Demond Hammond, Boobie Jacobs, Michael & Yolanda Jacobs, Ray Jacobs, Demetrius McClendon, Lamond Moore, Sean *Frisco* Moran, Threathere Pickett, Terry *T.P.* Prince, Debbie Ridley, Steven Ridley, Stephani Richardson, Curtis Schuler, Ambre Shaw-Sanders, Crystal Shaw, Izana Shaw, Shamar Shaw, Sharel Shaw, Messiah Sims, Charles C.W. Webb, Demarko

Weems-Hall, Ebony L. Weems-Mickel, Kishana Weems, Leonard Weems, Sheryl Rene Weems, Nakesha Whittle.

My warmest thanks to my wonderful editor, Terri Harper, for her boundless patience, understanding, sweet personality, and friendship; not to mention all her editorial experience and expertise.

And last, though by no means least, my warmest friendship is extended to Timothy R. Richardson and Delbert Smith for always keeping it solid with me.

If your name is not listed above, sign here:

_____

Eugene L. Weems

ACKNOWLEDGEMENTS

For the women in my life that keep me inspired and encouraged to remain aggressive about success. My mother, **Mrs**. **Yvonne Aubrey-McWoodson**, and my lovely and remarkably patient wife, **Mrs**. **Stephani Marie Richardson**. The both of you have become pillars of strength in my weakest moments, and beacons of light on my darkest days. And, for that, my hat is forever removed. Thank you.

To all of my children and the mothers who have raised and protected them in my times of absence, I commend you for your diligent patience and faith in me.

Lastly, but most important in my success as an author, I contribute unequivocally the full magnitude of my appreciation, admiration, and respect to hopefully a future life-long friend, Mr. Eugene L. Weems, for choosing to share his magnificent mind and treasured advice in all things business, and all things funny, and most of all, all dreams that are reachable.

To my loyal and good friend, Ronnie *Hassan* Wattley, keep your head. Sky is the limit.

I am truly a blessed man with the people I have in my life.

Thank God, most of all.

Timothy R. Richardson

AUTHOR'S NOTE

For argument's sake, I want you to assume that this is a work of fiction.

I want you to assume that everything herein is the product of an overactive imagination, exacerbated by long stretches of solitary confinement and everything that comes with it: sensory deprivation, arrested development, loneliness, boredom, or insanity.

Assume there's no such thing as other dimensions, time travel, or holes in the fabric of time and space; that the world you know is the only world there is.

Assume everything you learned from your parents or other family members and society is absolutely, one hundred percent true; that the way you were taught to perceive things is correct; that your religion, morals and values are right; and that those whom aren't like you or don't share your views are simply *wrong*.

Assume your race is superior to others; that your nation is essentially good; that those nations who don't like your nation are essentially bad; that war is necessary to protect your way of life; and that you have nothing to do with your government's policies and actions.

Assume you are living just the way you were intended to live; that you have achieved your full potential; that you are complete, happy, and content; that this is as good as it gets; and anyone who dares to envision something new or better is just pure *evil*.

And by any and all means, assume that life as we know it is the only life in existence similar to ours; that there is ...

Now, navigate the depths of possibility that you are wrong about everything. Dare to dream. Dare to explore every catacomb of your imagination. Or better yet, we dare you to journey with us to places that would challenge all that we as a human race have come to accept, acknowledge, and understand as *normal*.

Allow us to introduce *The Other Side of the Mirror.*

CHAPTER 1

George W. Bush was born with one goal in mind, to become President of the United States. It had been a long time and a vigilant journey, but finally his dream was going to become a reality. As he took a long glance at his handsome reflection and soaked in the moment of January 2001, so much had changed since his childhood days of growing up wealthy in the state of Texas and enjoying the lifestyle as the son of a wealthy oil mogul. He remembered the stories all too well of how the Bushes came to power and how his great, great-grandfather came up with the marvelous idea of importing African slaves. From cigarettes to cigars, the quality of Bush products was known throughout the world, with assets over $5 billion and products in every country.

Why would George W. Bush want to become President of the United States? It was simple, because it was what he wanted, and he usually got what he wanted. The unwavering desire to have it all served as his motivation. He once watched the Miss America pageant on his big screen plasma television, and a surprised Laura Welch from Georgia was crowned the winner. George made a few phone calls, organized a meeting, and enter the new Mrs. Laura Bush, a perfect trophy to show off to the critics in the political realm. She was drop dead gorgeous with a runway model build and crystal clear hazel eyes. It was love at first sight, at least for a lust-filled George. Ten years, five mansions, over $3 million in jewelry, and two children later, they were a textbook couple. I can think of over a billion reasons why any man would want to be George W. Bush. He was young, wealthy, powerful, and had a beautiful wife. The final cherry on top was his landslide victory over Al Gore and Joe Lieberman to win the presidency of the United States.

George had many accomplishments, was a Rhodes Scholar, Phi Beta Kappa, Yale University, youngest Texas state senator and CEO of Bush Enterprises. Everything had come so natural and easy. Money couldn't buy everything, but it sure purchased a lot for him. He had bought his way to the top and slicked more palms than the oil used to lubricate all the cars at the Indy 500. His philosophy was, *everyone had a price; they just didn't know how much.* He was arrogant, rude, self-centered, a male chauvinist, and of course as racist as a Confederate general. He was a political fox that could out talk the most experienced politician, and everybody loved the image George W. Bush paid to create. Women adored him and men admired him from a distance. He had a lifetime commitment from his public relations firm; negative portrayals of him disappeared faster than Michael Jackson's nose. He was America's golden boy, and now the first family was going to be treated like royalty.

The soon-to-be-President of the most powerful nation in the world took one more look at himself in the full-length antique family mirror. It had been in his family for generations, passed down from his great, great-grandfather, Winston George Bush. It had been rumored to be the luck of the Bush fortune. The very same mirror was passed down to George's father from his grandfather, and now it belonged to him. It was no secret that every male Bush had spent countless hours admiring their perfection in that very same mirror. It was now his turn to hold the family treasure, and he was in his prime.

He studied his features. His eyes, nose, facial features and chiseled physique. Carefully inspecting every inch of his body for any hint of imperfection. He marveled at his flawlessness. He was the same perfectionist that would stay in his mansion for weeks as a teenager, at the sight of a pimple. Now was his time to shine.

He looked every bit the part of a man in his mid-twenties. The skin treatments had worked wonders. It was now time to meet the vast audience that awaited their new American King.

Finally, he had to perform his daily ritual of kissing his reflection in the mirror. It was the only way that he knew how to start his day. He had tricked so many people, paid his way out of so many different situations, fooled even the most astute and highest paid lawyers. He had created an image of a demi-god in the media and throughout the land, but he could not fool the mirror.

The mirror showed the truth, and George hid from the truth. He could fool his wife, his kids, his employees, his political allies, and even 90 percent of the American voting public, but he could not fool the other side of the mirror.

One additional kiss for good measure as he departed to his awaiting audience. His beautiful wife Laura was waiting with his twin daughters, Barbara and Jenna. Everything had worked out perfectly; one strong family with perfect Eurocentric genes. The epitome of excellence, a true royal family.

Thousands had gathered for the celebration as George fulfilled his dream of becoming the President of the United States. Many thoughts went through his mind as he began his acceptance speech. After his initial thanks to his family, colleagues and numerous associates, he began to wonder if he hadn't bitten off more than he could chew. America was the most powerful nation in the world, and even George began to question his decision. So much was going to be decided by this President. Six new supreme court justices would have to be appointed, the issue of reparation for African Americans, a diminished Social Security fund, oil embargos by Iraq, communism in China, the reunification of Germany, the lack of control of the CIA and FBI, and the internal problem of the national debt. The rich wanted to stay rich; the poor wanted to be rich. So many problems and so little time to solve them.

George had his mind made up. He was going to be the greatest President ever. He was going to change the world. In spite of all his intentions to be the Kobe Bryant of the political world, he had to select a Vice President and a secretary of state out of the multitude of candidates willing to serve as his right hand.

He had selected his college roommate and trusted friend, Cheney Burrows, as Vice President and running mate. An absolute yes-man who virtually idolized George. He did not have the worry of Cheney stabbing him in the back, and he could always keep him in check.

The position of secretary of state was another story altogether different. He had to appease his African American voters, who had all but declared him the next John F. Kennedy. Mass consumers of his tobacco products, the African American women loved his young, educated white male look, almost straight out of *G.Q. Magazine*. His slick persona and hip talk had made him popular with the men. He even played the saxophone.

Although he deeply despised African American people, there was a strong push to keep them happy, so he reluctantly appointed an African American woman as his secretary of state. It was sheer genius, as he satisfied two critics with one appointment, African American voters and women's advocates. After a nationwide search, he had found the perfect candidate, Ms. Condoleeza Kincaid, a fellow Yale Law School graduate who was a popular news anchor for WGBN in Chicago.

She was also an *oreo* and married to Bill Kincaid, a white divorce lawyer. There was no secret to how she worked her way through law school and gained a reputation among the male Anglos at Yale, becoming their first African American sexual experience. The past was the past, and that was several years and several pints of tequila ago. Now Ms. Kincaid was a loving and almost committed professional wife.

All the other cabinet members would be the usual menial appointments. A Hispanic here, an Asian there, a few more women, and maybe somebody Islamic. President Bush wanted his cabinet to reflect his voting public. He was a real wolf in sheep's clothing and everyone was convinced that he was a messiah. Most of the critics loved him, and those who didn't were paid to like him a lot, the first candidate to run as an independent and win by a landslide. *A man of change* was his theme and you could hear the chants of "Bush! Bush! Bush!" from his millions of followers. At times, he would mistake the chants of "Bush" for "Lord" in his own narcissistic mind. He felt as if he were the people's Lord, a modern day savior, and they loved him.

It was a new day in the life of George Walker Bush. His dreams were finally made into reality, President of the United States of America, the most powerful country in the world, maybe even the universe.

Later on that evening, Cheney Burrows and his wife, Mary Ann were settling in for their first night at the official residence. The events of the day were still difficult for him to stomach. Butterflies still circled around mercilessly in the abyss of his soul. He was a total mess and still could not believe that he was the Vice President of the United States. He enjoyed his newly found status as the second most powerful man in the world. The aspirations that dwelled in his head were many. He was all too familiar with the trend of the Vice Presidents eventually taking the post of President, so he didn't mind playing second fiddle to Mr. George Bush. Besides, he relished the role.

Over the many years of their friendship, he was used to being second to George. If the President was Batman, it was safe to say that Cheney was Robin. There were a lot of perks playing second to a billionaire, and he graciously accepted them all. He did so with a genuine appreciation of all things granted to him by his lifelong buddy, George Bush.

They had been through so much together as roommates in college, George usually serving as the comet and Cheney the comet's tail. As youngsters, they were inseparable. Even in the many women George used like bathroom tissue, he usually got the prom queen and Cheney dated the chubby best friend. On more than one occasion, after George broke a beautiful damsel's heart, Cheney was there to gobble up the leftovers. He was not the handsome hunk that George turned out to be. In fact, he was the short and nerdy intellectual. There was not a subject in the world that escaped Cheney's knowledge. He was a walking Encyclopedia and had the IQ of a brain surgeon; the main reason that George kept him around, and everybody knew it. Cheney was not even remotely a threat to George's status and was as replaceable to him as a member of Mike Tyson's entourage. It was the looming potential of being expendable that kept Cheney on his toes. He wanted nothing to come between he and George. It was safe to say that George was his idol. Thus, the reason for him being appointed as George's running mate and become Vice President of the United States.

Cheney had worked hard to climb the ladder of success. The wealth in his family was the result of a state lottery ticket that his dad won when he was a junior in high school. The consummate student, he was always academically blessed but financially cursed. His father was a half-decent automobile mechanic in Chicago, Illinois. His mother, a beautician at a local beauty salon. He got all of his knowledge from spending countless hours with his grandmother, who was a former college math professor and had just recently passed away. There was a rumor that the Burrows' intelligence gene skipped an entire generation, and that was the reason he was so smart.

He had scientifically created a formula that came up with the six winning numbers of the Illinois lottery at 15 years old. Even his parents doubted the validity of his formula until one day a drunken Paul Burrows gave it a try. Twenty-seven million dollars and several years later, Cheney was treated to the finest education money could buy. Rumors soon circulated about his sudden rise to family fortune in his freshman year at Yale. He was an easy target for the senior ivy leaguers to pick on, and one day George came to his rescue. They have been friends ever since that day. George was the money and the power, and Cheney was his brains, a match that was made in heaven. George did not worry about the critics because his family was wealthier than all of theirs combined. But still, the route that Bush took to fortune and fame was vastly criticized.

Cheney had made a pretty good living for himself by being George's flunky. He had a decent-sized mansion, a few luxury vehicles, millions in his bank account, and now was Vice President of the United States. He even owed George for introducing him to his beautiful and wealthy wife, Mary Ann Jennings, the darling princess of the Jennings clan, owners of a multimillion dollar chocolate company. Few children in America had not tasted the pleasures of a delightful Jennings chocolate bar.

Mary Ann was spoiled rotten as a kid, and even worse as an adult. Her brief love affair with George was short and torrid, several sexual acts in discrete locations graphically described by George to Cheney. She was far too much of a slut to have ever been considered a housewife for him, but a perfect mate for Cheney. George hooked them up about ten years ago and they have been inseparable.

The only person as bossy as George was Mary Ann. Her demands were mammoth and her mouth was as big as the Grand Canyon. She was a real slave driver and she rode Cheney relentlessly. His self-esteem was as low as a doormat. Her criticisms of his refusal to stand up to George were endless. She criticized him for leaving his secure position as a member of the House of Representatives. She criticized his decision to remain loyal to George. She criticized his hair, the clothes he wore, and his attitude. It was safe to say that he believed her family was better than Cheney's family. She had never worked an honest day in her life and she knew all about Cheney's road to family riches. She did not respect him. The only reason she married him was to keep tabs on the antics of Mr. and Mrs. Bush. It was no secret that Mary Ann was still in love with George. Cheney tolerated it all and kept his opinions to himself. Over the years, he had become the consummate sponge.

Condoleeza Kincaid lived in a world of firsts. She was the first person in her family to graduate from college, the first African American woman to graduate from Yale Law School, and now the first African American woman to serve as Secretary of State. She loved being first. She had even cum first when having sex with her mate. No words could describe the feeling that she felt about being appointed Secretary of State. She was going to be on the cover of every magazine; *Jet*, *Ebony*, *Newsweek*, *Time*, *Sisters 2 Sisters*, *Essence*, and even *People*. She had finally made it to the top, the third most powerful person in the United States. She loved being in the spotlight. All of her years as a token had finally paid off.

She was still in shock about her nomination endorsed by President Bush and subsequent appointment. She knew that her qualifications were more than enough for the post, but her skin color had prevented her from entering the social circles of the Yale Law School elite. Many of the white males loved having sex in secret but would never be caught fraternizing with a black girl. George had never spoken more than two words publicly to her, but she was spotted a few times leaving his off-campus home. Cheney didn't even know that she was a Yale Law School student until the graduation ceremony.

So much had changed for her over the years. She had screwed her way to the top of the news chain at WGBN in Chicago. She went from the cute, little African American weather girl in the tight miniskirt to primetime news anchor, the most popular personality on the nationwide television station, first in her timeslot. Millions of people depended on her information and her image was omnipresent on the majority of televisions in America. Condoleeza was a household name; everybody loved her.

Needless to say, her marriage to Bill Kincaid, a wealthy white lawyer from Kansas, was on the rocks. They seldom had time for each other, there was not enough time in a 24-hour day. They had no intention of having children, so sex was a thing of the past. All in all, Condoleeza loved having her white, successful *trophy* to show off among her NAACP friends in social circles. Her happiness was safely in the hands of public perception, and everybody viewed her as being happy with Bill. She could conjure up a smile almost as fast as Diana Ross. Her pearly whites graced the pages of many magazines and televisions. Condoleeza was a socialite and wouldn't be caught dead without a smile on her face. Now she had the whole world as a stage, the perfect diplomat and politician for the most important position in George Bush's cabinet.

CHAPTER 2

The move to the White House was definitely a step down for President Bush and his wife, Laura. Several upgrades would have to be made for this luxurious billionaire couple. They were used to being waited-on hand and foot, usually by African Americans, because in George's mind, they made the most loyal servants. Their mansion in Texas was almost twice the size of the White House, with double the staff. Some major remodeling had to be done before George would feel comfortable performing his Presidential duties. He viewed his new surroundings as being inadequate despite the numerous changes that had been made. He knew that he was going to spend as little time as possible at the White House and that Laura was already missing their Texas mansion.

His first meeting was with Vice President Cheney Burrows in the Oval Office. The newly elected President sat at his desk with the American flag on the wall behind him. It was their first meeting together and Bush beamed with a glow of confidence. His Vice President sat there with a nervous look on his face, as if they had just hijacked the White House. "I'm going to need your undying support," President Bush declared with the confidence of a championship coach.

"Whatever it takes," Cheney said in response. Bush gave him a fatherly smile of approval. They knew that Cheney was his main man. He was happy that his Vice President was at his beck and call.

So many other agencies were against him; jealousy in the Senate, opposition in the CIA, FBI and the DEA. The alphabet soup of American politics was a mixture of so many organizations with so many functions that it was impossible to pay off everyone. Vice President Burrows was going to be his political watchdog. Even President Bush knew that he was going to need help governing the most powerful country in the world. There were so many issues, so many campaign promises, and he was not going to lose his position as the new American messiah. The image of his country had taken a severe blow and the deficit was at an all-time high. All of the countries in the world were depending on him to change things around for the better. He had made bold and powerful moves as the CEO of Bush Industries, and his loyal followers expected nothing short of a miracle during his tenure as President. Now was the time for America to regain its position as a worldwide power, despite a $20 trillion deficit.

He pressed a button at the end of his desk, and seconds later, an African American uniformed servant appeared, "Yes, Mr. President?" Benson the butler inquired as humbly as possible. George ordered coffee, and within seconds the steward disappeared.

It was time for them to get reacquainted. "How's the family?," Cheney asked, as if to break the silence. He knew the answer to the question before he even had the nerve to ask. He knew all about the royal family and the immense demands of Mrs. Bush. She couldn't possibly be happy with the move to the White House and the departure from her Texas palace.

President Bush went into a long tirade about the inadequacies of the White House. Cheney listened intently to all the details and knew that he had opened the flood gates. The steward returned with a silver tray, a pot of coffee, and two cups, each imprinted with the Presidential seal. He skillfully poured the coffee, "Can I get you something else, Mr. President?"

"No, thanks," he said, and gave him a glare of discomfort. The steward took it as his cue to get lost and exited the room.

The President then continued his conversation with Cheney. He described the duties that came along with being the Vice President, how important it was for Cheney to maintain a short leash on the CIA and FBI. He demanded that his Vice President keep a watchful eye on anyone who was against his presidency. It was very important that his position be held in the highest regard. He wanted to be the best President ever, the people's messiah. For the first time, he acted as if he needed Cheney. George Bush was a master manipulator and

15

knew exactly what he was doing. He needed the mind of Cheney working for him behind the scenes. He was the face, body and spirit, but he needed the mind of a genius to persevere.

These two men had engaged in many conversations before, but somehow this conversation was on a different level. George spoke with power and the voice of a unbridled leadership. He was powerful and very persuasive. Cheney was almost in tears. A new bond was developed, even more solid than the previous relationship the two men had shared. So much had changed in the heart of George Bush. He was fearless and charismatic. The spirit of all the Presidents in past dwelled inside of him. Cheney had a new appreciation for the spectacle that was taking place before his eyes. He liked everything about George Bush. He loved his best friend and now blindly supported him. He committed himself to his President's every effort, whim and demand. After hearing George speak as President of the United States, it was safe to say that Vice President Cheney Burrows was willing to die for his Commander in Chief.

The transition to power for Mrs. Bush was not going quite as smooth. There were too many items and not enough space for the First Lady. One of the first items to go back to their Texas mansion was George's family vanity mirror. Laura was never told the legacy of its existence, thus looked at it as a worthless piece of furniture. Every single inch of space in their master bedroom was already accounted for, mostly with her belongings. She cursed the former First Ladies for such a small area. There was no way that she was going to survive for four years in the White House, and re-election was out of the question. She commanded the movers like a drill sergeant barking orders. The White House had never seen a person who demanded more. Nothing was satisfactory. So much had to be done. She had to find tutors for the children, hire more maids and butlers, organize dinner parties, and find a beautician. Life was so much easier in Crawford and it would have been a simpler task to have George pay to have their mansion moved to Washington. It was going to take a miracle for her to adapt to life in the White House.

Secretary of State Condoleeza Kincaid made her move easily, like a thief in the night. Somehow, she had talked Bill into staying back in Chicago to take care of things. She was a free woman, ready to paint the town. Freedom she had only dreamt about was now at her fingertips. Her position as Secretary of State was going to give her the opportunity to travel the world at the expense of the government. It was heaven on earth. So many places to see, so many people to meet. She was going to be the most recognized Secretary of State, ever. She looked forward to meeting the leaders of the world on behalf of the President. She looked forward to making her boss look good and was determined not to let him down.   He had made an excellent decision in appointing her.   She was intelligent, beautiful, dedicated, and able to mingle with the social elite.   She had a familiar face that many world leaders had seen before. The magic of television had reached even the most primitive societies.   It was s dream appointment with all the trimmings. She had settled in her condo in no time at all. It was finally time to relax and celebrate a bit. She couldn't remember the last time that she had a decent orgasm, so she grabbed the thick yellow pages, looked under the long list of escort services and did a little shopping for male companionship.

CHAPTER 3

Vice President Burrows didn't waste any time in getting to know the people under his command. He knew that his job was to play the background while the President was in the public eye. He realized that someone had to do the dirty work of maintaining democracy and recognizing any enemies to America. He was the perfect man for the job. He hated anything that was not Anglo Saxon male, and held high ranking in the Illinois Chapter of the Ku Klux Klan. He was in strong opposition of President Bush's appointment of Condoleeza Kincaid to Secretary of State, but he would never question the decision of his fearless leader. He was too much of a coward. Few people truly knew of his blatant dislike of anyone that wasn't white. He was the perfect candidate to head the branches of federal intelligence. He had made his way to the CIA Headquarters and was in a closed-door meeting with Donald Prescott, Director of the CIA.

It had already served to be an eye-opening experience for the Vice President. The public was never admitted inside of this building. Few even knew of its existence and there were no facilities for visitors. His entrance was through a long tunnel that emerged into a closed room protected by several suited guards. The entire episode seemed like a scene from a science fiction movie. Cheney immediately recognized that he oversaw a powerful tool in American government, international intelligence. He had an entire army at his beck and call. They could eliminate anyone from existence, violate the privacy of anyone in the world. It was all up to him and the President to determine who the enemies were and point a finger in their direction.

Cheney loved his position of power; Donald Prescott answered to him. He was higher on the chain of command than the director of the CIA. Director Prescott addressed him as *sir* and shared intricate details of the many secret missions going on throughout the world. Cheney had done his research and knew all too well about the exploits of the agency. The power was in his hands now and he was ready to abuse it. He and the President had came up with a list of names and organizations that they wanted fully investigated. They wanted to combat terrorism and anyone who threatened democracy. The first name on the list was Dr. David Lee Phillips, an African American lawyer who was creating a lot of noise about African Americans receiving reparations. Second was Muhammad Abdul Wail, an Arab activist from Arizona. Third was the UBN, United Blood Nation, a street gang that was more powerful than any organized criminal gang that America had seen. The list had over 40 handpicked individuals selected by the President and Vice President.

Cheney smiled as he looked down the list and quickly added Condoleeza Kincaid, Secretary of State. The future of American intelligence was in good hands. He was already giving commands and setting deadlines as if he were President. He was already abusing his power. The only person in America that he had to answer to was George Bush. He was glowing in confidence and a new sense of power that had been a stranger to him for far too long. He liked being in control. Now he knew why good Vice Presidents became decent Presidents. It was only going to be a matter of time before he had his opportunity to run the nation. He could live with his role as a follower because he knew that one day he would eventually take the lead.

After a long week on the road spent lobbying for various amendments, staffing the remaining cabinet vacancies and pledging to fulfill campaign promises, President Bush was finally back home in the White House. He exited Air Force One and entered the White House under the close protection of his Secret Service men. He arrived inside his sleeping quarters in desperate need of rest. So much was on the young President's mind. The movement for reparation spearheaded by Dr. David Lee Phillips was gaining support. It was to the point where it was moving to the forefront of issues important to the President. Even in all of his fame and

21

fortune, he could not afford to lose the African American vote. His appointment of Condoleeza was the perfect pacifier, but now his African American supporters were hungry for real food.

Something had to be done, but there was no way that he was going to stick to his campaign promise of establishing a trillion-dollar reparations fund for the ancestors of slaves. He was not prepared to bless African American people with that much financial power. He laughed at the thought of coons running wild in society, buying up all the Cadillacs and gold chains. Chaos would rule their neighborhoods. He figured that all the money in the world couldn't turn their plight around and regretted his decision to support the reparations bill.

He noticed the lack of space in the White House sleeping quarters. Laura had brought so much junk from their Texas mansion and 80 percent of the items belonged to her. As he went through the clusterfuck, he realized that many of his belongings were missing. He wondered where they had disappeared to. He had never slept in a room so small and had never travelled without a full moving crew. He hated sleeping away from the luxuries of his mansion and especially missed his daily ritual with his family vanity mirror. It was his security blanket and his source of good fortune. He could not go for more than a week without re-energizing in front of the vanity mirror.

He went through all the items carefully this time, making sure that he did not overlook anything. He

22

became upset when he realized that his family vanity mirror was gone from the location where he had directed it be left. "Laura," he yelled, his voice echoing throughout the White House.

A sleeping Laura was startled and feared the worst. She knew of Bush's rampages. He could become very brutal on a moment's notice. His philosophy was *spare the rod, spoil the wife and child.* On several occasions, he had become physically abusive toward her and the children. She knew from his tone that this was one of those occasions. "Yes, honey," she replied as meek as a sheep.

"Where is my mirror," George calmly asked.

Laura almost lied, but instead she opted for the truth, "I had it shipped back to Texas."

The President was overcome by a fit of anger. His eyes became red with fury from his soul. The love for his wife was immediately robbed by the hatred that filled his heart. In a chain reaction, he slapped Laura silly without hesitation. He grabbed her by the neck and choked her until she was on the verge of passing out. Then he tossed her aside like a ragdoll and stormed out of the room. Laura curled up into a ball, fearing continued assault. She was safe for the moment, as President Bush made his angered exit to Air Force One. He had one destination in mind, his Texas mansion.

Many thoughts went through his mind as he de-escalated from the incident with his wife. He wondered how a woman so beautiful could be so damn stupid. It was an obsession for him to be able to admire himself in the mirror. It was as much a part of his life as his wife and children, the sun, the sky, the moon, and even the air he breathed. To think that she shipped it back to Texas without a second thought made him so angry. He was not going to tolerate impertinence, especially from his wife and children. He was a devout Atheist with no belief in God. In his opinion, man controlled his own destiny. He would soon see how wrong he was.

The Vice President had an extremely busy week fulfilling his duties while the President was away playing diplomat. Somebody had to maintain the security of the country and keep tabs on the many turbulent situations emerging. Even with his genius, Cheney had trouble juggling the social, economic, political, religious, agricultural and business concerns. It was mind boggling. The past administration had not made any progress, but he was going to come up with the answers even if it killed him. He was a workaholic with one goal in mind, proving himself to President Bush.

He also did a little political positioning of his own after he realized his new sense of power. He was overseer of both the FBI and CIA. The directors of both organizations had to answer directly to him. The power of the strongest intelligence gathering forces in the world were at his disposal, unlimited power to make anyone he desired public enemy number one, and he was going to utilize every single ounce of it. Cheney was really beginning to smell himself. So much power in the hands of a once powerless man could turn out to be extremely dangerous.

He glanced over the most personal details of the lives of every single person on the list he provided to CIA Director Prescott. He knew that he had access to two very powerful tools. Information was the most important weapon in civilized society and he wanted it all. He could record all phone calls, have vehicles identified, monitor bank accounts, check employment history, have every second of your day monitored, and even have your home invaded. Just one phone call and a simple phrase, "I believe that he's a terrorist." To make matters worse, his jurisdiction was worldwide. He could not believe that so much power was granted to one man. He could make a person disappear from existence or die from a sudden heart attack. Cheney Burrows had come a long way from the scary nerd people once bullied in school. Now he was all-knowing, omniscient, with destruction at his fingertips. He was Vice President of the United States.

In the luxury of her spacious condo, Condoleeza savored her newly found freedom. She relaxed in the confines of her Jacuzzi, naked, glowing and sexually satisfied. The luxury of privacy had been a stranger to her for far too long. So much had changed in her life with her appointment. She had already scheduled her first political visit to France. It was going to be a wonderful tenure being a diplomat and having entire countries cater to her every whim. Actually, the President had not done bad in his appointment. She was an excellent speaker, sexy, and articulate. Many world leaders would love to try and seduce her into their beds. Condoleeza was going to take this opportunity to meet and greet the wealthy, and with a little luck, maybe she could find a new husband.

After all of the years of hard work, she had finally been accepted into mainstream America. So many of her African American brothers and sisters had labeled her a sellout, but now she was getting the last laugh. She had made it out of the ghetto and now rubbed elbows with the political elite while the same bitches that criticized her became dependant on the welfare system. White America loved her and had accepted her as one of their own. She was rich, sexy, and as close as possible to being white, the most politically powerful woman in the country. She had a green light to see the President with any issue that her heart desired. Victory was hers and Condoleeza was going to get as much as she could while the getting was good.

CHAPTER 4

President Bush had finally touched down on the landing strip of his Crawford, Texas, estate, over 1400 miles from the White House, and he was glad to finally be home. His anger still boiled toward his wife and he was grateful for the distance between the two of them. Finally, he had the opportunity to spend precious time alone with his mirror, but two tall and muscular Secret Service Agents followed him like a shadow. He already had plans of forcing them to post up at the front entrance of the estate and protect him from predators.

Cheney had designed the security system himself and there was only one system like it in the world. It was owned by Ahmed Akbar, a Saudi Arabian oil billionaire, and he paid twice as much for his installation. The Gladiator Fortress was impenetrable, a complex combination of sonic traps and infrared detectors controlled from a satellite hundreds of miles overhead. No thief in the world could come within a mile's radius without being detected. George controlled the entire system from the confines of his Rolex watch. It was the

27

ultimate in high-tech gadgets and his Texas estate was in good hands.

George was going to enjoy his time alone with his vanity mirror. He was like a compulsive gambler who had not made a wager in months. He missed the beauty and perfection of the solid gold frame and almost mystical reflection it produced. It was more than a vanity mirror to him. It was the mirror to his soul. Many times he would stare, hypnotized by the imagery displayed in the mirror. It was vivid and real, and he would talk to himself for hours and hours. He was his worst critic and had shared so many secrets with his vanity mirror. It was his best friend, his closest confidant, and soothing therapy for his fragile mind. Nothing gave him more satisfaction than being able to talk to his own image. It was how he planned his day, contemplated his future, and handled all of his insecurities. He loved his vanity mirror because he was vain.

As he made his way to the rear entrance, he saw a sight that he could not believe. He saw this vanity mirror in a large box outside, near the service entrance. He was outraged. It was like a rare and precious jewel left laying on the ground of a New York subway. Although its frame was solid gold with diamonds of all colors, the stones were so huge to the average person they might be considered to be fake. George could not believe that his wife had been so careless with such a priceless possession. She was going to pay dearly for her idiotic mishap. If she only knew the history of the mirror, she wouldn't have dared to be within a thousand feet of it, more or less, than to have it removed out the place of safety. George's ancestor had stolen the mirror from an African tribe when they invaded the tribe to collect slaves to bring to America.

He ran quickly toward the tall box and greeted it like a long-lost love. He carefully cut open the box, almost desperate to see if any harm had been done to his vanity mirror. He was amply relieved that it was still intact, as flawless as the last time he had viewed its perfection. Everything was in its proper place and it glistened in the sunlight. He quickly ordered the two Secret Service men to carefully take it upstairs to his suite. George closely supervised the move and made sure it occurred without incident. Once completed, the agents were ordered outside and George was finally alone with his vanity mirror.

Privacy at last, he had a lot of making up to do. He immediately grabbed one of his imported towels and began the process of his cleaning ritual. The thought of strangers handling his most prized possession made him sick to his stomach. He was beyond upset with Laura and was almost to the point where he wanted a divorce. Calmer heads would prevail once he realized that as a leader of America his personal life was an open book. The President of the United States of America could never divorce the First Lady, no matter how stupid she appeared. His vanity mirror shined like new money and almost met even his high standards. As he viewed his crystal clear, full body reflection, he was in love again.

The gold shined like the morning sun and the image that was in the mirror was an exact replica of his perfection.

He had so much to share with his vanity mirror. His last conversation with himself was at the White House, after the inauguration. So much had changed. The metamorphosis took place almost instantly. He had changed from one of the wealthiest men in the world to the most powerful man in the world. He was officially the President of the United States. He had the power to start a world war, the power to appoint lifetime judges to the Supreme Court, to create and cancel laws that ruled the land. No single man outranked him, everyone was under him. He was the Commander in Chief, the Chief Executive Officer, and the Head of State.

George Bush loved the way he looked in his vanity mirror. The spirits of his ancestors were proud of their native son. No other Bush had reached such lofty heights, no other Bush had been so famous and noteworthy. He was immortal and would go down in history as the first Bush to become President.

He glanced at his reflection and began his conversation with the image in the mirror. He talked about the issues burdening him. His pitiful wife, spoiled children, and the incompetence that surrounded him daily. He bared his soul to his vanity mirror and it listened intently. He studied his reflection and marveled at its splendor, so handsome, so smooth, so articulate and so omnipotent. He talked on about his position of authority, how wonderful he was, and how great it was to be George Walker Bush.

As the conversation escalated beyond the level of conceit, it became therapeutic. It was an episode of intense verbal masturbation. Nobody had ever thought so much of himself. The more he talked the deeper he fell into an abyss of self-glorification. In his view, America needed him in this time of crisis. No President in history could measure up to his dashing good looks, political charm or stunning personality. He was the ideal President. The compliments flowed like a river. "I am wise, worldly and wonderful. I am here to protect and save America. I will be remembered as the messiah that saved the world. I'm great. I will create so much. Come to think of it, I am their God. I am god. I am God!"

He approached his reflection and kissed the vanity mirror. The mirror began to shake and the image of his reflection turned into a black man. It was a black version of himself. Handsome, same height, weight and physical build. George couldn't believe his eyes and was stunned beyond belief. Was it too much talk about reparations? Too many days on his feet?

He stumbled away from his vanity mirror. His mind was playing a horrible trick on him. He went over to his bar and prepared himself a tall goblet of Hennessey XO. He drank it like bottled water. Before it had reached the bottom of his throat, he poured another cup, and another, and another until, eventually, the entire contents of the bottle was gone. He wanted so desperately to remove the image he had seen. George Bush could never picture himself as a nigger. A spear chucker, a coon; not George

Walker Bush. It was a brief nightmare that drove him to the point of opening yet another bottle of Hennessy XO.

He eventually drank himself to a stupor. He sat alone in the luxury of his massive bedroom on his expensive designer leather recliner. He was still in disbelief. He needed a break, but the sensation of intoxication had overwhelmed him. The horrible reflection was a distant memory as he glanced in his vanity mirror and saw the purity of a white face. He began to laugh to himself, almost hysterically, as he thought about the image of him being black. It was funny as hell, a place that he would one day call home. But for now, he sat there, calm and relieved.

Eventually, he gathered up the courage to make amends with his vanity mirror. He figured that maybe the mirror had gained a personality of its own and decided to punish him. Maybe it was his ridiculous campaign promise of supporting the reparations bill and giving a trillion dollars to African Americans for 200 years of slavery. Finally, he just realized that he had spent too many hours in his mirror adoring himself. He was pleasantly intoxicated and exhausted from all of the events of the past week. It had been one hell of a rollercoaster ride, and that was just the beginning.

He gathered himself, took a long, hot shower, and changed into his pajamas. He stumbled over to his mirror to begin his customary ritual again. He looked at the blurred image in the mirror, a fraction of the man who had just become President. He was still in love. His vanity was not permanently damaged. The self-gratifying compliments began to erupt out of his mouth again, like lava from a volcano, "I am handsome. I'm the most powerful man in the world. I can buy anything or anybody. Everyone has a price; they just don't know what it is yet. I am God. I am God. I am..."

He was close to his reflection, almost kissing his image in the mirror. The reflection changed to the black image and snatched his body through the vanity mirror. George was startled as he emerged on the other side of the mirror, as if he had been pulled through a time warp. He was magically transported to another place and time. He was no longer in the confines of the country he ruled. He was introduced to his version of hell.

He glanced around his new environment and saw a lavish master bedroom almost as wonderful as his, but slightly different. It was a room fit for royalty. Fine beautiful and exquisite furniture was in every corner. It stretched the length of a professional tennis court in both directions, east and west, north and south. In the place where he entered, behind him was a marvelous vanity mirror that rivaled his family mirror in its beauty. It was almost identical in its features. He analyzed the texture of the gold frame as it sparkled magnificently. He walked over to the solid oak dresser and noticed the spread of fine, exquisite jewelry. Rolex watches, diamond rings, emeralds, and a jewel-encrusted crown. It was like a fantasy come true. He picked up the watch to inspect its quality, an exquisite Presidential Rolex. He tried it on and it fit almost perfectly.

"Stop, thief! Security! Security!" a voice shouted that stunned George. Within seconds, two tall, black, muscle-bound men, figures worthy of being defensive linemen in the NFL, emerged through the entrance. George was instantly taken down with a banned WWE move. He had never experienced such pain and was used to being on the giving end. The restraint left him motionless and powerless. He lay there in awe and wondered who in the world had the audacity to order someone to place their hands on the President of the United States. Somebody had some serious explaining to do, and fast. He looked up for an explanation and another black man stood tall and powerful over him. He was regal in his demeanor. His eyes strained but finally focused and made out the facial features. He could not believe who he saw. It was the black man that appeared in his mirror.

A powerful surge of energy went through George's body. His entire being was consumed by fire and he felt excruciating pain from the top of his head to the bottom of his feet. The princely figure was the last figure George would see, and afterwards there was darkness. The two black men handcuffed his hands and applied ankle chains to his motionless frame. They then carried his body away like weekend baggage. President Barack Obama wondered how a servant had passed several guards and made his way into his living quarters. His security minister, Solomon, had some serious explaining to do. His fortress was impenetrable, millions had been spent on his protection. The Black House had never been infiltrated.

President Barack Obama felt violated. A white man had touched his possessions and had invaded his privacy. So much had changed since the whites had been released from slavery so many years ago. Blacks had tried so many things to get rid of them, even genocide. *Those wretched whites are like roaches. They are everywhere and serve no purpose.* Something had to be done to prevent this from ever happening again, even if he had to make an example out of that intruder to prove his point. The newly elected President had a lot of housecleaning to do. He was the leader of the most powerful country in the civilized world, the Republic of Acirema.

Two entire days had passed with no word from President Bush. The two Secret Service agents posted out front became worried beyond belief. Agent O'Neal finally got the nerve to enter the mansion and made his way to the door of the master bedroom. He knocked gently at first, "Mr. President?" No answer. Seconds later, "Mr. President?" Still no answer. He feared the worst. He pulled out his semiautomatic weapon and blasted the locks in an attempt to gain entrance through the steel doors. He was successful as he kicked the door from the large hinges. He was inside the master bedroom and the room appeared vacant. There were no signs of a struggle, just a neatly piled wardrobe and a Rolex watch. "Mr. President?" He called out, praying for a response, but there was no answer. He searched the closet, the bathroom, and even underneath the bed. He noticed no signs of forced entry. President Bush had mysteriously vanished.

Vice President Burrows was disturbed by a phone call, "Mr. Vice President, President Bush is missing," a breathless voice said.

Cheney was in shock and did not know what to do. He hoped that it was some cruel inhumane joke by the President to test his loyalty. "What do you mean, he disappeared?" The Vice President demanded an immediate explanation.

"He's gone," the voice muttered in defeat.

"Who is this? Where are you calling from? What is the meaning of this game?" Cheney was in no mood to display a sense of humor.

"Sir, this is Agent 005, Peter O'Neal. We escorted the President to his Texas estate and he is missing."

There was a brief silence. "I want your ass to meet me at the White House ASAP. I don't know what kind of games you Secret Service people are playing, but I want answers." He slammed the phone down with a hostile authority and its plastic casing cracked it in several places.

Cheney was fuming and confused. How could the leader of the most powerful country in the world just up and disappear without his personal Secret Service bodyguards knowing his whereabouts? It just didn't add up. It's unheard of. He had just met with him a few days ago. Cheney had installed the security system himself. Something had to be wrong. Somebody had made a grave mistake. How do you lose track of the President? Heads were going to roll.

Cheney quickly retrieved his cell phone and dialed the phone number to George's Texas estate. No answer.

He quickly called the private line at the White House. After several rings, Laura answered, "Yes, George," she hoped, speaking in an apologetic voice.

"Sorry, Laura, it's me Cheney." He could feel the disappointment. "Is the President available," Cheney said.

"No, he's been gone for the past two days. I believe he went to Texas," she said in response.

"Thanks. Sorry to interrupt you," Cheney said, avoiding further comment until he had a chance to get the full story from Agent O'Neal.

He exited his house and dove into the back of his Mercedes Limousine while his driver drove like a madman in the direction of the White House. A pain appeared deep in the pit of his heart for his missing friend. He cared deeply for President Bush. His love for him was borderline obsession. A million thoughts went through his mind as his vehicle surged on through the traffic. How could the President have vanished from thin air? Somebody knew all of the answers. Many scenarios circled through his recollection. Maybe it was a horrible joke, maybe the President had a mistress, maybe he was hiding somewhere within the confines of his massive

Texas estate, maybe he was underneath his bed. Cheney was dumbfounded for the first time. He did not have the answer to any of the questions.

Soon he was within the gate of the White House and he cleared security. In no time at all he was in the large briefing room and several concerned faces were already there awaiting him. "What the hell is going on," he barked to a silent crowd. All eyes were on the Vice President now, making it impossible for his entrance to go unnoticed. The most powerful people in America were there and they all stood bewildered and tongue-tied. CIA Director Prescott, FBI Director Richardson, Joint Chief of Staff Admiral Striker and Secret Service Head Bob Smith, Vice President Burrows outranked them all. It was at this time he realized the magnitude of his power.

In the absence of President Bush, he was the acting Chief Executive Officer of the United States. He was all powerful and he was the HNIC (Head Nigga in Charge). He began to like being in charge. The power to intimidate powerful leaders became a welcome drug to his system. He wanted his authority to last. He rampaged on, "I want answers! All of your asses are on the line. I have never seen such incompetence." The room remained silent.

CIA Director Prescott broke the ice, "We have agents combing every inch of his Texas estate. We have questioned Mrs. Bush. Nobody knows anything."

Next, it was Secret Service Agent Smith, "My men reported the incident and we still have no leads. No signs of a struggle."

"That's ridiculous! That's absurd! Nobody just disappears into thin air," acting President Burrows said in the direction of the two men.

"That is my account of what happened, sir," Agent O'Neal said in response.

Cheney approached the agent like a raging bull and slapped him with mighty force. He then grabbed the agent by the collar and yelled, "You find George and you'd better find him soon!" Agent Smith quickly came to his deputy agent's rescue. Nobody abused CIA agents without his consent. Cheney Burrows realized the error of his ways. A leader could never be seen in public losing control of his emotions. He released the agent, gathered himself, and realized that he had an audience.

He regained control like a proven politician. "How will we explain this to the American public?" The most popular President ever was missing. He had disappeared without a trace. The tabloids and news media are going to have a field day with this. "We have to do something and do it now." The urgency of the situation had taken on a new meaning.

Cheney headed for Air Force Two with Agents O'Neal and Jones. They were headed to the Texas estate. The two agents would receive additional questions during the flight. He wanted every single detail of the President's disappearance from the two men who saw him last. Secret Service Agent Smith described Agents

O'Neal and Jones as two of his best agents. Cheney had never seen such incompetence, and serious upgrades were already being thought of for the Secret Service Academy. He could not believe that the President's protection was left in the hands of such idiots. No wonder so many Presidents had been assassinated.

They touched down on the landing strip and the two agents were sweating from the vicious interrogation on the flight. Cheney was out of his seat before the jet had come to a complete stop on the Texas estate landing strip. He knew that the security system at the President's estate was impregnable. He had installed the system himself and nobody got past the Gladiator Fortress. He did not have a clue as to what was going on, but somebody was going to have to pay for this absolute travesty.

The three men stormed into the Texas mansion. There were several members of the CIA and Texas branch of the FBI already present. Cheney found the lead investigator, Paul Winston. He received a briefing on their findings and there were no new developments to report. He escorted Acting President Burrows to the master bedroom. Nothing had been touched. Cheney quickly grabbed the Rolex watch from the dresser and examined it. After a brief look, he knew that it was George's watch. It was the exact same watch that he had programmed for the security system years ago. He knew immediately that something was seriously wrong. The President loved his watch and he would not have been caught dead without it.

He scanned the room and everything was in place. No sign of a struggle or forced entry, aside from the massive door removed from the entrance. Cheney was even more confused. It was unlike George to disappear unannounced. He liked being the center of attention too much. Something had to be done fast. He quickly called CIA Director Prescott and organized another meeting with the top officials in the Executive Branch of government. He was going to need some time to figure out his plan of action. He ordered Paul Winston to have everyone removed from the mansion. He demanded that everyone be sworn to secrecy and that anyone who leaked information would face severe punishment. He spoke with bad intentions and nobody doubted the seriousness of his statement. Within minutes, the room was empty.

After a few more minutes, the entire mansion was empty. The acting President stood in the room alone, holding the diamond-studded Rolex watch of his closest friend. He was already missing him dearly. All of a sudden, he was gravitated toward the vanity mirror on the north side of the room. A strange feeling overcame his person as he glanced at his reflection in the mirror. He knew that something was wrong and he was going to figure out what it was. Nobody could disappear from the face of the earth, especially the leader of the most powerful country in the world. Nobody would be foolish enough to kidnap the President of the United States. He used every ounce of his extensive brain power but still could not rationalize what had taken place.

He glanced around the room one more time, hoping that his lost friend would appear and yell out, "Surprise!" Unfortunately, he stood alone in the utter silence. He was frustrated beyond belief and began crying tears of intense pain. For the first time, he was without his protector and ally. He felt alone for the very first time since he was a child. He could not believe how things had gone so horribly wrong. In a burst of confidence, Cheney gathered himself, looked into the mirror and said, "I am going to find you, old friend. I don't care what it takes. Even if I have to comb every inch of this planet, I promise that I will find you, George Bush, even if it kills me."

George Bush awoke in a prison cell, alone and still in shackles. After a few moments, reunited with his senses, he realized that the episode from earlier was not a dream. The pain that was still present throughout his body confirmed the reality of the entire episode. Every part of his person throbbed in agony. He had never experienced so much pain. He still did not know where he was or how he had managed to get there. Somebody had some serious explaining to do. Who was that mysterious black man? How dare they place their hands on the President of the United States. He reached for his cell phone that he kept in his coat pocket. He realized then that he was in his bathrobe. He had never seen the inside of a prison, but he knew that he was entitled to a free phone call. He would then call Cheney Burrows and settle the entire situation.

He heard the noise of heavy footsteps coming in his direction. They stopped directly in the front of the entrance of his cell. "All clear, Cell 12," said a deep soulful voice, and the door magically slid open. Two unformed black men came into the room and told George to get up on his feet.

"This way," the tall, black, muscular man said, pointing in a direction leading down a long hallway. George feared for his life, so he humbly complied. He struggled to his feet and walked painfully down the hall. He noticed several other uniformed blacks walking in the hallway. He had never seen so many black men and women in uniform.

As he walked down the hall, he glanced into the jail cells that lined the walls. He noticed that all the occupants were white inmates. Immediately, he thought he had been kidnapped by some African nation, but he did not recognize any accents. Their English diction was totally American and the atmosphere was far too advanced. He was then led through a steel sliding door into a dark room where he was pushed into a seat at a table. "Lights," one of the guards barked. The room was immediately illuminated. The two guards departed and George was left alone with handcuffs and ankle chains attached to his body. He glanced around at his new environment that seemed like some type of torture chamber or interrogation room. The walls were padded and appeared to be soundproof. He wondered who could possibly have been behind this crime, and why. He was terrified and willing to pay every penny of his $3.5 billion for his freedom.

He heard more footsteps heading toward the room and two black men in fine designer suits came walking through the door. One took a seat at the table across from George; the other remained standing. The one that was standing stared at George like he was nothing, a worthless piece of trash. The one that was seated seemed calm and collected. He smiled pleasantly and introduced himself, "I'm Special Agent McBounds, National Security of Acirema. Who are you and where are you from?"

George could not wait to identify himself, "My name is George Bush, President of the United States."

The two men burst into near hysterical laughter. George felt as if he was at the wrong end of some kind of joke. The sitting agent finally gathered himself and said, "But seriously, who are you and where are you from?"

"I'm George Bush, newly elected President of the United States."

This time, a more serious atmosphere prevailed. It was obvious that the joking mood was temporary. The atmosphere had turned serious. The standing agent said, "There is no such country. The United States? A white man never could be elected President of anything. You are insane!"

George avoided eye contact. The standing agent was all business and he did not want to argue with him. He sat in silence for a minute and then said, "My name is George Bush and I'm from the Unites States of America."

The two agents were still puzzled and gave up all hopes of an intelligent conversation. The seated agent then said, "Okay, George, what were you doing in the President's bedroom?"

George realized that he was fighting a losing battle and was not about to tell them the story of what actually happened. "I don't know," he said, and this apparently set the unidentified agent off. He approached Bush and brutally slapped him in the mouth. It was a punishing blow that made Bush see stars. Blood trickled down the side of his mouth and he felt violated.

"No more games," he yelled, "We want answers!"

Bush just sat there, shaking nervously in fear of another attack. He didn't know what they wanted to hear and he searched his mind for the right answers. He would have said just about anything to avoid being pimp slapped again. Several thoughts lingered in his mind as he thought of some type of logical solution to his problem. He wanted the whole episode to end and to go back to his life of luxury at home in Texas.

The barrage of questions from the two men continued and George finally gave up. He figured the best thing to do was to give no answer at all. He didn't want to fall victim to any more physical attacks, and his plan worked. Eventually, the two stopped. Finally, Agent McBounds said, "We are charging you with ten criminal counts and you're facing a sentence of 125 years. Do you have money for a private attorney?"

Bush was relieved; he had plenty of money. He just needed to call his wife in Washington D.C., "May I make a phone call," he asked with a new sense of confidence.

Agent McBounds un-cuffed his hands and handed him a slim cordless phone. George looked at the numbers on the keypad and they appeared foreign. He had never seen symbols like that before, nothing close to American numbers. He thumbed-in the symbols where he recalled the numbers on an American phone would be located and hoped for the best. No connection. He tried it again, but no luck. The standing agent smirked, then snatched the phone from his hands. George sat there like a school boy being disciplined. It was a living nightmare and he had never felt so hopeless.

So much had changed in such a short period of time. He went from the most powerful leader in the world to a situation of hopelessness. He had lost all of his worldly possessions and contact with everyone who had ever loved and worshipped him. His life had been perfect, and now he wondered what had caused this recent turn of events. How did he end up in such a horrible place where nobody knew of his greatness? He was a leader, a man of great wealth, and almost a God. George wanted to end it all and contemplated suicide for the first time. Any sort of afterlife would have been an improvement to his present situation, even the eternal fires of hell.

Two weeks had passed since the disappearance of President Bush and Vice President Burrows was worried beyond belief. The story that the President was sick and in bed at his Texas estate was beginning to lose its credibility. The rumors had already began to circulate, and despite his power as acting President, he still could not stop the freedom of the press. The public was tired of the picture that was being released to the media. They wanted to see a live image of the President. People in several circles around the country feared the worst. The television talk shows and tabloids added fuel to the fire with their assumptions of what happened to the President. One London tabloid had reported that he had been abducted by aliens. Another source said that he was on a secret vacation with Elvis. The stories continued to pile up like Pete Rose gaming chips, each one more sensational than the last. Vice President Burrows had to do something about the hype, and soon.

There was still no word about the President's disappearance. Just one lead had turned up and it wound up being a silly prank from a bunch of college students at University of Nevada, Las Vegas. The Vice President was desperate and had even ordered CIA Director Prescott to comb the nation for a stand-in for the President. He figured that somebody in this country of over 500 million people had to have a similar build and facial resemblance to President Bush. He could serve as a visual pacifier until the real President returned. Cheney was running out of time. Even he knew that an imitation stand-in would work for only a brief period of time. Nobody in the world could match the charisma, style and pure arrogance of George Bush. The President was one of a kind. He had to come up with a master plan that would work in the long run. He sat in the Oval Office and the genius of his mind worked overtime coming up with a solution. He was the mastermind behind Bush's rise to power and glory. He was the one who made all of the decisions for him. He was the person who had helped Bush pass every exam he had taken since he was an undergraduate. The most powerful nation in the world was about to take a serious blow to its ego. How could America ever recover from a President disappearing into thin air? What would that say about homeland security? Nobody would ever feel safe if the President came up missing. Who could be next?

Cheney Burrows tried desperately to devise a plan. His thoughts were interrupted by a ringing telephone. "Vice President Burrows," he said,

"Mr. Vice President, we found your man. He's a cowboy from Oklahoma. His name is Jim Irvin," CIA Director Prescott announced triumphantly.

"Is he a perfect physical match," the Vice President asked almost in desperation.

"As perfect as perfect can be. The two could pass as Siamese twins," Prescott replied with a wry smile in his voice.

"I want to meet him immediately," the Vice President said, and made the mood serious again.

"It's a date," the agent said.

The two conspirators hung up the phone almost simultaneously. Cheney leaned back in his leather chair, a bit more relieved after his conversation with the CIA director. He knew the President better than anyone, and if anyone could train somebody to act like Bush, he could. The second phase of the plan was already being orchestrated in his diabolic mind. In the few weeks as acting President, Cheney had grown comfortable in his new role as Commander in Chief. Besides, if something else had to take his departed friend's place, he thought it might as well be him. He rationalized his decision with all of the work that he had done in the shadows while George Bush lived in the limelight. He had his mind made up and couldn't wait to meet cowboy Jim Irvin. The nation was in total chaos and the climate was as intense as any wartime situation. In fact, the Vice President viewed the episode as an act of war, and in war there were casualties. More than a few good men gave their lives to protect America. Thousands of people have died to protect American democracy as we know it. In his eyes, what difference would it make if we lost one country boy from Oklahoma if it cured the problem in the White House?

Condoleeza Kincaid had just finished another black tie event sitting for the President. These days, her calendar was stuffed like Thanksgiving turkey. She had at least two events scheduled a day. She predicted her position as Secretary of State would keep her busy, but this was totally ridiculous. She had not talked to the President in weeks and started to worry. The questions about his health and well-being were becoming more frequent with each engagement. To make matters worse, the only person he had talked to was the Vice President, and he did not keep his dislike for her a secret. On more than one occasion she heard the "N" word come out of his lips in reference to her. The feeling was mutual. Cheney was one of the few white men that she had not slept with. She viewed him as a coward and kiss-ass to President Bush. The only reason he had made any progress was because of his relationship with Bush.

Less than a month and she was already growing tired of her post. She needed a break and the journalist in her wanted some serious answers. It was more than she had bargained for. Her dreams of worldwide vacations had been shattered. The fact that she had to deal with Cheney on a daily basis made matters worse. The media darling enjoyed being in the spotlight, but it was a little too much attention for even her. She wanted to do her job and prance happily across the globe, not tend to countless questions about the President and his secret condition. She wanted him to do the job he was elected to do. Her instincts told her that something was desperately wrong at the White House and she was going to get to the bottom of what it was. She knew that Cheney was up to something, but he would never confide in her. The George Bush that she knew would never avoid the public eye, even in terms of sickness. Something was terribly wrong in the White House and Condoleeza was determined to get to the bottom of it.

Laura Bush had not seen her husband since the day he almost strangled her to death. She was beyond the point of worry. George had disappeared before for weeks, but he would usually take time to give her a call on the telephone. He would usually phone her with some kind of ludicrous request or demand to fulfill. George loved bossing her around. She had to admit that deep inside she enjoyed being able to roam around without a leash.

In secret, she wished that he were dead so that she could enjoy his multimillion dollar estate alone. She already had her first vacation around the world planned out, but she could never let the world know her true feelings. She was being watched around the clock by the Secret Service and the CIA. The government was treating her like a common criminal. She wanted the invasion of her privacy to end. Her woman's intuition told her that there was something wrong; she just could not pinpoint what it was. Cheney Burrows spoon fed her information from time to time, but nothing concrete. She never trusted him and she didn't like his opinionated ways. She thought that maybe her husband was on some type of top secret Presidential mission or just spending time away from her to cool off after his last episode. Either way, she was enjoying her break from his constant scrutiny.

The kids were already used to their dad being gone for long periods of time. They had all but accepted their

African American nanny, Mabel, as their surrogate mother. She had practically raised the two of them since birth. George spent too much time funding bribes, greasing palms, and running all of his many companies to be much of a father. Laura loved pampering herself too much and felt that she had done more than her share of work as a parent by giving birth to two children. The act of giving birth twice had almost permanently damaged her runway model physique. She thanked the devil for the miracle of modern day cosmetic surgery. She was on a first-name basis with her cosmetic surgeon and had gone through every procedure in the book.

She was in no big hurry for George to make it home. She savored the moments he spent away and loved being in control. She could be herself when she was alone but had to put up a front whenever her husband was around. Mrs. Bush longed for the day when she no longer had to play that silly game anymore. She wanted to be free. The only thing that kept her around was the promise of unlimited wealth, a little pain every now and then for a large amount of pleasure later. George often would get angry and call her a high-priced whore. She didn't mind because the wounds from the beatings and verbal abuse would all heal in time. She knew that in the long run that she would get the last laugh, all the way to the bank.

CHAPTER 5

President Bush was still trapped in a crazy maze where he had been brutalized and sentenced to 125 years in prison. It seemed like a horrible nightmare that he wanted to end. He could not believe the rate at which his life had deteriorated before his eyes. Nobody believed the story about being pulled through a mirror, not even his cellmate, Ken. He had traveled the world and he still could not remember any country by the name of Acirema. It had become his worst nightmare turned into wild reality. Blacks controlled everything, the police were black, his public defender was black, the judge was black, and even the President of the country was black. Of all the places to enter this mysterious place, it had to be in the President's mansion. Home invasion was a very serious crime in Acirema, especially if you were white and broke into a black person's home.

He had learned so much about the country from his cellmate. The colorful history of the country and how white slaves were brought from halfway across the world and sold into slavery. The slaves worked the land for over 400 years but eventually gained their freedom. Today, millions of whites were forced into the roles of second class citizens. The votes of whites who were fortunate enough to vote only counted as half a vote. Blacks and whites never shared the same public facilities, not even public restrooms. Blacks lived in the wealthy suburban areas while whites lived in the ghettos and housing projects.

Any political leader that emerged in the fight for white rights was either assassinated or placed in jail for life. White people never had it so bad, and the few that did make it assimilated into black culture. Ken gave George a thorough education on life for whites in the Republic of Acirema. George found it very hard to believe. When he told him about his country, people labeled him insane. The mere thought of blacks in an inferior role was subject to great criticism, even from his white colleagues. How did things go so wrong so fast? He looked for an escape route, but none was available. He wanted to take his own life but was in a padded cell on suicide watch. Every route that he thought about to freedom led to a dead end.

George had never been to jail before, not even for one night, and now he was cursed for 125 years for a simple crime like home invasion. He had a new found appreciation for his wife and children. He would never again enjoy the luxuries of being able to travel or running his businesses. He had no special privileges in prison. The sweet sensation of privacy was a thing of the past. There was a walk-through security check every hour and his cell was shook down every other night. His heart ached for the freedoms of home. Prison took away everything. One hundred, twenty-five years? A harsh punishment for a crime where nobody was harmed and all of the President's property was returned. The judicial system in Acirema was a fucking joke. Whites were hopeless victims to a system that blacks controlled, taken away from their families with no chance of rehabilitation. It was a cold game and for the first time George Bush was on the losing end.

Vice President Burrows met in the closed confines of the Oval Office with CIA Director Prescott and Joint Chief of Staff Admiral Striker. FBI Director Mike Richardson was not admitted because of his race. Cheney did not want an African American man involved in this highly confidential meeting. He had given up all hopes of the President's return and had constructed a plan. The plot to see Jim Irvin as stand-in had succeeded and the American public believed every word. The video footage of Irvin in bed, apparently sick with the flu, waving to his American public, received rave reviews. The President received thousands of get well cards and hundreds of flowers.

Cheney's plan worked, but now he had to find something more permanent. The demands to see the President started to build beyond his control. Dr. David Lee Phillips of RNF, Reparations Now Forever, was at the forefront of this movement. He questioned the validity of the President's sickness and publicly criticized the entire administration. He had gathered a large following for his call for reparations and had millions of supporters behind him. Something had to be done.

Vice President Burrows tried on several occasions to train Jim Irvin to act like the President, until finally he realized that it was a lost cause. Jim could never be President Bush. Cheney had come to the ultimate conclusion that he was going to have to sacrifice one life to save America from the crisis of a President that disappeared into thin air. It was easy to use Jim Irvin as a pawn in this game because he already knew too much about the President's disappearance. They could not trust him going back to Oklahoma with such sensitive information. The three men agreed that there could be no more leaks. Operation Phoenix was in effect.

Poor Jim Irvin, less than a month removed from landing at Washington's Dulles Airport and being announced as the winner of the lookalike contest, he thought the $100,000 was prize money. Jim was happy and the money would last a lifetime in Oklahoma City, Oklahoma. He was a man of very little needs. As he boarded Air Force One, he was surrounded by Secret Service agents and waving to his adoring public. He lived out his dream, being President of the United States of America, if only for a few hours. The Vice President had briefed him on his final reward, a face-to-face meeting with the President at his Texas estate. Jim couldn't wait to meet the President to thank him. President Bush was his idol.

Jim Irvin had made it safely on the plane. He took his seat in the passenger compartment and noticed that he was alone, without bodyguards for the first time. He didn't pay it any mind as the lone pilot greeted him, "Good morning, Mr. President."

Jim smiled and responded, "Howdy." The pilot began to taxi the plane down the runway. Soon they began to ascend into the clouds. Jim hated flying, but he realized that it was the way that city slickers traveled. It was only his second time on a plane. Finally, they reached cruising altitude and Jim decided to take a nap since the journey to Texas would take about three hours. He was awakened by a loud disturbance and witnessed the pilot free falling from the plane. He wondered what was going on in front and couldn't believe his eyes. He quickly arose from his chair and went to the cockpit. He stood in shock, the pilot's seat was empty. Jim feared the worst as he struggled to control the plane. It began to rapidly descend toward the ocean. After the pilot's parachute had deployed, he pulled out a small control device and pressed a red button. In an instant, the C-4 in the cockpit exploded. Air Force One went up in a thunderous explosion and Jim Irvin was no more. Operation Phoenix was a success.

Secretary of State Condoleeza Kincaid had just stepped out of the shower when she received the news,

"President Bush dies in plan explosion." She looked at her television screen in disbelief, stunned and speechless for the first time in her life. Tears began to trickle down her eyes for her dear friend, George. How could things have gone so wrong so fast? George had enjoyed a perfect life, and now this strange twist of fate. He was the only reason she took the wicked turn into the political limelight. President Bush was the only man who had enough courage to take the risk of appointing her to the post of Secretary of State. If George was dead, that meant that Vice President Cheney Burrows was going to be the new President, and there was no way she could work for him. Life was so unfair, she thought, the good people always died so young.

Her mind was made up and she had already began the process of packing her things to return home to Chicago. She wanted to get as far away from the Washington area as possible, she was quitting her post as Secretary of State. The phone rang and interrupted her thoughts of escape.

"Who is it," she asked.

"It's Vice President Burrows," the voice humbly responded.

Condoleeza was shocked at his passive tone. She had never heard Cheney speak to her politely. "What do you want," she questioned.

"Well, I just wanted to inform you of the funeral arrangements for next week. George would have wanted you there." The invitation almost seemed genuine.

"I will attend the funeral, but I'm surrendering my position as Secretary of State. I can't work with you."

Cheney sensed sincerity in her voice. "Listen, Condoleeza, I know that I have been mean to you since the day I met you. I want to call a truce between us." Cheney was so believable, showing hints of human emotion for the very first time.

"I..I don't know what to say," Condoleeza responded, confused by his sudden change of heart.

"Be my new Vice President, Condoleeza," Cheney offered, after a brief silence.

"Yes, Cheney, yes." Condoleeza considered for only a short moment.

The two former enemies then talked like long lost friends. Cheney blamed his cruel treatment toward her on his past insecurities, and Condoleeza said that she envied him for his close relationship with George. Eventually, they agreed to leave the past behind them and move on with their lives. Condoleeza found it hard to believe that she was talking to the new President of the United States. The conversation ended on a very positive note. Before Cheney hung up the phone, he said, "Congratulations, Mrs. Vice President." Condoleeza was on cloud nine. She hung up the phone and began to unpack.

President Cheney Burrows tried unsuccessfully to hold back the disgusting taste in his mouth. He could not believe that he had stooped to such a low level, where he pledged his support to a nigger, but it was the only way for Operation Phoenix to become a success.

After the meeting with CIA Director Prescott and Admiral Striker, they agreed that it would be best that he break the news to her. He wanted to select Senator Herman Lee from Texas as his Vice President, another redneck Klansman from the south, but CIA Director Prescott warned him that the nation would be in chaos if he passed over Secretary of State Kincaid for the post. After a brief argument, Cheney had learned his first lesson in politics. The CIA was far better at covering up political scandals than he could ever have been.

They unanimously agreed to give Condoleeza a watered-down version of the Vice-Presidency. She would have no authority over the CIA, FBI, or any military leader. She would simply serve as a political diplomat and just a pretty face in the White House. They knew that access to the confidential historical data stored in the CIA could prove to be very dangerous, especially in the hands of a former journalist. Her political appointment as the first African American Vice President would make America forget all about the tragic death of George Bush. It was the perfect smoke screen. Prescott had taken Cheney's plan to a whole new level. President Burrows could have his cake and eat it, too. *Why not, ain't that what it's for, to enjoy the sweet sugar dish?* He would remain in control of the CIA, FBI, and the entire military force of America. He could appoint his ally, Senator Lee as Secretary of State, thus have no reason to communicate with Condoleeza. The public would love him and he would have absolute power.

Cheney had finally prevailed over good looks. The inadequate nerd from rural Illinois had finally prevailed over the wealthy brat from Texas. It was a revolution more stunning than Kobe Bryant stealing the Lakers from Shaquille O'Neal. It was a total turnaround. Cheney Burrows was now President of the United States. He also had control of the most powerful intelligence-gathering forces in the world. Cheney was finally at the top of the political food chain after so many years of lurking in George's shadow.

Laura could not believe the news as it flashed on every channel simultaneously. She had never felt so lucky. George Bush was finally out of her life. The President was dead. She frantically flipped through the channels on her big screen television and each one confirmed the news of the explosion. She wanted to jump for joy, dance a jig, and scream, "Hallelujah!" No more physical abuse, no more verbal putdowns. She finally had an opportunity to raise her children the way she desired. She knew that George had no will. He thought that he was going to live forever. The entire Bush fortune was hers. Finally, her patience had paid off. Laura Bush was in control.

She knew that she still had a bit of role-playing to do, the funeral ceremony and the signing of all the transfer documents, mere formalities, to her becoming the richest woman in the world. Her darling American public would love and cherish her throughout history as the poor widowed First Lady. She already had her crying techniques perfected. Acting was the skill that had won her the Miss America title. She acted like she enjoyed being married to George Bush. She acted like her life with him was perfect. She had done so much acting over the years that she forgot who she really was, a spoiled and confused country girl from Georgia who was in awe of the lifestyle that a billionaire lived. She was no longer star struck. Having everything meant nothing without true love. She was tired of the media invading her privacy, tired of being told how to walk, who to talk to, and what to eat. She was tired of being called stupid and fat, and now she was finally free.

"Mommy, is daddy dead," a young voice questioned from the hallway without even the slightest hint of sadness.

"Yes," Laura responded, not knowing what to expect from her daughter.

"Good, now we can move on with our lives," the young girl said to her mother's approval.

"Don't talk that way about your father," Laura responded in a half-hearted attempt at defending her fallen husband.

"I'm glad he's gone, too, no more beating," the other twin's voice added to the conversation.

"Your father is dead and we have to move on with our lives. No more conversations about him." Laura gave unchallenged directives to her children for the first time. The twins stared at her in disbelief, as if they had seen a total stranger. "Go to bed now!" The twins retreated to the safety of their rooms.

Laura loved the newfound sense of authority. The children had nobody to run to and tell of their verbal abuse. George was not there to overrule her authority. So many times she had given the kids orders or tried to discipline them and George would overrule her decision, but not this time. Nobody was there to tell her what to do or how to raise her children, and it felt great. Laura had the final word and was finally taking back control of another human being. It felt good to be free.

The funeral had all the popularity of the world saying goodbye to an American idol. Everybody who was anybody was present. The entire nation was shut down for a day. It was an unofficial national holiday. The festivities would have made George himself proud, including a 21-gun salute with all the trimmings. Cheney Burrows held in his jubilation that his plan had worked out magnificently. He held in a smile of satisfaction as he served as a pallbearer for the lookalike for the man everyone thought was his best friend. He had successfully fooled the entire universe. He marveled at his superior mind. It was filled with brilliant ideas. He had pulled off the perfect master plan, and when the smoke finally cleared he was going to be the most powerful person in the world.

The first family showed the appropriate amount of sadness. Jenna cried her eyes out while Barbara was solemn. Laura cried tears, too, but unfortunately they were fears of unbridled joy. She was happy to be free from his vile clutches. Now she could finally live her life in peace. The Bush Family was as tight as ever, despite the absence of their ruthless dictator. So much had changed in such a short amount of time, and the change was as welcome as the morning sun. After all the years of living a lie, finally things were working out for Mrs. Bush. With each shovel of dirt tossed over the closed casket, a piece of her past was being buried until finally her soul was free.

Condoleeza Kincaid was sad for the departure of a friend, but thrilled with the opportunity that evolved as a result of his death. She liked George Bush, but she loved the idea of becoming Vice President of the United States. She was already beginning to admire Cheney Burrows for recognizing her leadership qualities. Who knows what could happen next. Maybe she would wind up President of the United States. The sky was the limit, anything was possible. George's untimely death was all part of God's plan. In time, he would eventually be forgotten. Needless to say, nobody would ever forget the first African American Vice President of the United States, Condoleeza Kincaid.

While Jim Irvin was being given a hero's sendoff at home in America, the real George Bush was suffering in the prison of a foreign planet. It was chow time, lunch. For lunch, a greasy slice of bologna, a half pint of milk, an apple slice, and two slices of bread, a small buffet to a preschooler, but hardly enough to satisfy the appetite of a grown man. He hated his new environment and cursed God for his misfortune. It had been almost two months and nobody had come to his rescue. He hated Acirema and the racist regime that held him captive. Ninety percent of the inmates were white. He slept on a sponge mattress and wore the same prison jumpsuit for weeks. He had no money on his books and the only hygiene materials he received came in the form of an indigent kit: a small bar of soap, a comb, two sheets of paper, and a stamped envelope. He wished for a razor to cut his throat and bring about an end to this living hell. The letters he sent to his Texas estate returned *No such address*.

He could not believe the world he had been thrown into. Everything was backwards. Blacks controlled the economic, social, political and financial power. They made up 95 percent of the prison staff and even the warden was a black man. During dayroom, on television they dominated every channel and owned every station. In the newspapers, they received headlines in the world news, sports and entertainment sections. The only portrayals of whites on television were negative, violent crimes, lootings or robberies. A white President had never been elected in Acirema during its history. All of the books were about blacks, even the comic book superheroes. Somebody had placed George Bush in a cruel game and had gone to incredible lengths to make it seem real.

He wanted to call the police, but his call for help would go unanswered. He wanted to post bail, but his money was not within his grasp. He had no family, no friends, and for the first time he was all alone. His freedom was stripped away from him without any representation in a court of law. Sentenced to 125 years for home invasion? A prison system where a judge gave out prison sentences like McDonald's sells hamburgers. Inmates were abused by the prison guards constantly. Your every move was monitored and you were counted daily like cattle. George wondered, how could a place so horrible exist in such a powerful country? He was absolutely powerless for the first time in his life.

George was not going to settle for his present situation. He had to figure his way out of Acirema, even if it killed him. Death would have been a more joyous fate than 125 years in prison. A simple mistake was not going to cost him his life. For the first time in his life, he regretted treating his wife so cruel. He wished that he could take back all the harsh words he had said to her in attempts to assassinate her character. It was all out of his reach now. He had to live with his reality. He wanted advice from his pal, Cheney. He knew that he would be able to find a way out of this situation. He was more determined than ever to find a way out and was not going to rest until he found his way back home.

The White House lawn was filled to capacity as Chief Justice Goldberg inaugurated the next President of the

United States, Cheney Burrows. He was met by twice as many followers as President Bush, a tribute to this new found sense of popularity, the first President with enough courage to appoint an African American Vice President. Cheney's popularity among the American public was at an all-time high. The white conservatives loved him and knew of his undying support of the Ku Klux Klan. They realized that Condoleeza Kincaid was a token appointment.

Senator Herman Lee was the real Vice President. He was Cheney's right hand man.

The explosion of Air Force One left no traces of Jim Irvin's remains and the entire world was fooled into believing it was the President boarding that plane. Cheney, Agent Prescott and Admiral Striker were the only three people on the planet who knew the secret of who died in the explosion. He now had the power to run the nation the way he wanted. He was going to use his power and influence to become filthy rich and lay in bed with wealthy lobbyists.

Cheney glanced out at his loyal followers as if he were destined to be President. He was now highly visible to an approving public and backed by powerful white friends. He began his acceptance speech.

"I come out of the shadows to accept my position as President of the United States. I accept this position in honor of my best friend, George W. Bush. I accept the torch of leadership of America, my version of America. I plan to take back this country from the terrorists who took away our President and brought about the 9/11

tragedy. Today I'm announcing a war on terrorism. I
pledge that we will find and destroy all who stand
against our freedom. God bless America. God bless the
United States."

A loud eruption of applause emerged from the
clueless crowd. They accepted every word that their new
President said as gospel. He had never been so adored.
He accepted his new popularity with the passion of Julius
Cesar. A great sense of confidence filled his spirit. He
was small in stature but stood as tall as a giant.

His wife, Mary Ann Burrows, looked on in
admiration of the man her husband had become. All of
her coaching had paid off. She finally had a winner. For
the very first time, she was proud to be his wife. So
much had changed in such a small amount of time. She
found him sexy for the very first time since she had met
him. No longer was he a useless tool that she used to pry
into the life of George Bush. She no longer envied Laura
for being the First Lady. It was her time to enjoy
success. Her husband had finally made it to the
forefront. He was the President and she was the new
First Lady. She was going to enjoy running the White
House.

The transition went as smooth as a baby's bottom. It
was a new day, America had a new enemy. The whole
incident was blamed on terrorists and now the President
had the green light to wreak havoc on whoever he chose.
Who was a terrorist? Who was an enemy of the State?
The enemy was so vague, so difficult to describe. What
was the difference between a law-abiding citizen and a

terrorist? The power to judge was safely in the hands of the Sons of Liberty, the new secret organization comprised of President Burrows, Secretary of State Lee, and CIA Director Prescott.

Eugene L. Weems, Timothy R. Richardson

CHAPTER 6

President Burrows had a new backbone and had more political power than any single person in the nation. The Sons of Liberty were here to stay, a top secret branch of nationwide white supremacy opposed to anything or anyone who stood in the way of confederate ways. After their meeting, they decided to target Dr. David Phillips and end all possibility of keeping the ridiculous promise of accepting a reparations bill for African Americans. It was something that Cheney had severely opposed, but there was no way that he could ever have let George Bush know his true feelings. Now that he was in command, things were definitely going to change. Now, with the support of his new organization, he was going to turn back the hands of time. He had a new vision for America, a new hope for the future, and it most definitely did not include reparations for African Americans.

Douglas Winters, a staff reporter for the *Chicago Tribune*, knew that something fishy was brewing in Washington D.C. and it had Cheney Burrows written all over it. He had followed the Bush administration and produced several articles on the Vice President. His relationship with him dated all the way back to his early days as member of the House. Doug was intrigued with Cheney from the very beginning and followed him from the day he used George's money to buy his seat in congress. He traced the two political hotshots all the way back to their days as college roommates at Harvard.

Doug's infatuation with the two men had turned into a full blown addiction. He could not get enough of writing about the two men, but something more was troubling him. He kept rewinding the footage of President Bush boarding Air Force One on what turned out to be his final trip on earth. He kept focusing on the scene of the President waving to the crowd prior to boarding the plane. He watched carefully, studying the scene as it played out again and again. Something was wrong and he couldn't quite figure it out.

Suddenly, he vaulted out of his chair with excitement, "That's it," as if he had solved the mystery of human existence. He barged into the office of Carl Watson, the editor in chief.

"I found it," he said in triumph.

"What," Mr. Watson said as if he had better things to do.

"I knew that there was something strange about the footage of President Bush boarding the plane," Doug explained.

"And?" Mr. Watson was a man of few words. He wanted to know the facts.

"Well, I met George Bush during the Presidential debates and he gave me an autograph, and then shook my hand," he further explained.

"What's the point," Mr. Watson said, urging Doug along.

"In the airplane footage, President Bush is waving with his left hand," Doug explained.

"So what, that's not unusual." Mr. Watson was losing his patience.

"President Bush is right handed." Doug looked at Mr. Watson in the eyes and smiled.

A few hours later, Doug was on his way to Washington D.C. with a new angle. He didn't have a lot, but he had talked Mr. Watson into giving him two weeks on the story. He was seldom wrong about his hunches. He knew all about Cheney Burrows' association with the Ku Klux Klan. He knew about Herman Lee and his affiliation with the Klan also, but the appointment of Condoleeza Kincaid as Vice President was a mystery. Doug had a hunch that something was terribly wrong at the White House and he was going to get to the bottom of it.

Laura monitored the movers as they moved the last of the belongings back into the Texas estate. It was a long and tedious process getting settled back in. She was happy to finally be back in her home. The lawyers had filled out and she had signed all of the paperwork regarding George's estate, and Laura was now officially the owner of over $3.5 billion in assets. Being a billionaire was a sweet sensation for her. She felt as if she had earned every cent of it, putting up with George for almost 15 years. She was finally free and able to breathe without being suffocated by the demands of her marriage. She was going to enjoy life to the fullest.

At last, she was alone in her lavish master bedroom suite. She looked around at the expensive imported furniture, the antique lamps and signature paintings. Everything was safely in the same place, just the way George had designed it years ago. She thought about contacting the interior decorator but realized that she did not have to worry about the return of her nagging husband. It felt good to have a permanent vacation from his mood swings. She almost didn't know what to do. The feeling of peace was still new to her. She no longer had to act like a queen. She no longer had to put up the front of being more than mortal, a walking goddess without human emotion. Without George around, she no longer felt the urge to order people around. The desire to give orders turned out to be a vicious domino effect, beginning with George, passed to her, and down to the end of a chain. Nobody was there to order her around anymore. She was now in control of her life, her home, her future, and her dreams.

The funeral was over, but Laura still felt his presence. She desperately needed closure. She wanted to be rid of everything that reminded her of her ex-husband. She began by gathering up his belongings, his clothes, belts, shoes, pictures, golf clubs, and anything that belonged to him. In a fit of rage, she began several long treks back and forth to the backyard until an enormous pile of his belongings was created. She kept adding and adding to the pile until all memories of George were out of the bedroom and piled into an impressive heap in the yard. Laura felt an increased sense of freedom with each item that was removed from her home and added to the humongous bundle. She was freeing her soul as he took gasoline from the garage and soaked the remnants of her past.

She went upstairs to her bedroom and checked thoroughly one last time, but nothing remained. She looked at her reflection in the mirror, a mere shadow of the young damsel who was selected as Ms. America. She was so far removed from her humble beginnings in Atlanta. Her life was spent starving herself on special diets, maintaining a paper-thin figure, because her husband repeatedly called her fat. It had been over 10 years since she tasted the flavor of her mother's homemade apple pie.

"No more lies," she said, in a personal confession that her body accepted as a welcome release. "No more lies."

She repeated it like a mantra. The burden was removed. For the very first time in years, Laura Bush looked in the mirror and liked what she saw. She took one moment and looked at the beautiful woman she saw in her reflection and smiled a genuine smile that made her cheeks hurt. Her mood changed instantly when she realized that it was George's vanity mirror that she gazed into. In one fluent motion, she grabbed a brass vase from the table and tossed it into the mirror. The vase connected to the mirror, causing an explosion that sent fragments of glass everywhere. Laura felt a sense of relief knowing that there would be no retaliation, no complaints, no beatings, and no George Bush to punish her.

She turned to exit her room and yelled, "Children!" The twins came to meet her with puzzled looks on their faces, "Let's go get some pizza," Laura said with a smile. The two children smiled together in relief, their prayers had been answered. They gathered into their Rolls Royce and Laura left the kids in the car with one item of unfinished business. She returned to the large pile in the backyard, lit a match, and said, "No more lies." She tossed the match into the pile and watched the flames devour the remnants of her past. Without further thought, she sighed a long sigh of relief, smiled, and returned to her awaiting vehicle.

As the car made its way down the long driveway, Barbara turned and said, "Look, mom, the house is on fire."

Laura turned calmly to her and said, "Don't worry, honey, we're rich. If it burns down, we can buy another."

The three of them laughed like never before, true happiness for the first time. It was sad that the children had lost their father, but in the process they gained a mother.

Meanwhile, in a prison in Acirema, George was awake at 5 o'clock in the morning, sitting at a stainless steel table with seven other inmates. He stared at his tray in hope that the objects on it would somehow change in structure to resemble food. Breakfast these days was a dry biscuit, half a cup of cornflakes, half an apple, and half a pint of milk, a gourmet meal to an inmate at Acirema Correction Facility. George had once tried to avoid eating but eventually gave in as starvation settled in. He had a newfound motivation to escape. It took several weeks, but he had convinced his cellmate of the existence of the United States.

At first, Ken thought he was a lunatic just like many of the other inmates in prison, but after a while, George had won him over with sincerity. George also promised to make him a rich man if he helped him to escape. All George needed was the support of one man for his cause. Before he knew it, rumors spread like wildfire. In no time at all, he had a small army at his beck and call with Ken as his lieutenant. The class of whites in this country were very easily influenced. They needed something or someone to believe in, and George was the perfect messiah. His dashing good looks and law school vocabulary thoroughly impressed them all. Anything was an improvement on their hopeless lives in Acirema. George spoke of a place they had never seen before, not even in their wildest dreams, a place where whites ruled with an iron fist, a place where whites lived in unlimited wealth, in big houses fit for kings and queens. He told them about the history of his world, white leaders, like Hitler, Stalin, Caesar, and George Bush, men of power who brought war to the doorsteps of anyone who opposed their philosophies.

Every day, the audience got larger and his influence grew more powerful. Kites were being sent throughout the prison describing this bold new leader, a fearless man who spoke about blacks in a negative tone that they had never heard before. He used insane descriptions, like savages, spear chuckers and jungle bunnies, terms normally used to describe their race throughout white history in Acirema. He told them about the continent, Africa, where blacks suffered from disease and famine. The whites believed it was impossible that a place like that could ever exist. All of the places blacks lived in Acirema were beautiful and spaciously modern. Blacks ruled all civilized societies and held all of the positions of power. All of the books and documentaries of their history showed their legacy in detail.

To his surprise, the words George spoke were often met with harsh criticism by many of his white colleagues. He was amazed at the self-hate and the overwhelming sense of hopelessness that was prevalent among his people. He grabbed a prison dictionary and thumbed through it until he found what he was looking for, *"White. Having no light; evil; cheerless; lack of color."*

George could not believe his eyes. He quickly thumbed back to front of the Acirema dictionary, *"Black. Pure, good; holy; to make clean."*

He continued looking up derogatory terms, like *white male, white wash, white market,* and *white ball.* All negative connotations. He began to see the reasons for the poor self-esteem among his people. It was as if they were brainwashed. At that point in time, he realized the extent of the damage that had been done. Their lives were beyond repair. He was going to use the small support group that he gathered to gain his escape and get as far away from Acirema as possible. He had to figure out a way to get back to America and he knew that the pathway led through the mirror in the bedroom of President Barack Obama.

Vice President Condoleeza Kincaid sat alone in her office and looked over her calendar of activities. It was a watered down version of her duties as Secretary of State. She had fallen for the *okie-doke,* the oldest trick in the book. It was what whites did to all African Americans when they needed tokens. The President had just appointed her to a higher position but had taken away all of her power and authority. She was a paper title, a false idol without power of control over any government agency. She was just another pretty face in the White House, a traveling façade. Condoleeza had made a deal with the devil and she had come out on the losing end.

She felt stuck between a rock and a hard place as she stood in her office, undecided. She could not give up her position as Vice President; too much was at stake. She was deceived into accepting the post and now the entire world knew. She could not resign under any possible circumstance. Her picture had graced the covers of *Time*, *People*, *O*, *Newsweek*, *Essence*, *Jet*, *Sister 2 Sister*, and *Ebony* magazines. She represented hope for black America. If she quit her post, African American progress would be set back hundreds of years. Who knew when there would ever be another opportunity to have an African American Vice President. So much was on the line and so many people looked up to her that she couldn't possibly resign.

She'd had only one meeting with President Cheney Burrows during the past two months as Vice President, but Secretary of State Lee met with him at the White House on a daily basis. He practically lived at the White House. He and President Burrows were always in some type of top secret, closed-door meeting in the Oval Office while Condoleeza was sent continent hopping, campaigning for support on the war on terrorism in America. She called the President with complaints, but her words fell on deaf ears. Condoleeza was running out of patience and something was going to have to change. Her journalistic intuition was getting the best of her. Condoleeza Kincaid may have been a slut, but she was far from being a dummy. Something fishy was going on in the White House and it stank all the way up to the Oval Office.

CHAPTER 7

Cheney sat at his large desk and could not believe an article that he read from a contributing journalist in the Washington Post, "President Bush still alive?" It was an article by Douglas Winters. It uncovered the plot to fake the President's death in detail. The only tidbit of information missing was the real President Bush's whereabouts. The story was too close for comfort and something had to be done. Rumors were beginning to circulate about Condoleeza being a token appointment. Dr. David Lee Phillips had developed a strong presence in the media and demanded that President Burrows honor the promise made by former President Bush to fund the reparations bill. He couldn't satisfy his wife sexually and even Viagra wasn't working. His problems as President of the greatest free country in the world continued to grow at an alarming rate.

President Burrows almost wished to return to his position in the background, or at least to the comforts of his Illinois senatorial position. America was a big country with even bigger problems. Why did George Bush have to disappear? What happened to all of the power in the White House that he was supposed to have? Who was going to lead the way now that his leader was gone? Who was he going to turn to for direction? Burrows was in the uncomfortable situation of being forced to make final decisions alone. He had failed to realize that with unlimited power also came unlimited responsibilities.

He searched his mind for solutions. He realized that the Douglas Winters story had no true merit and was based on the reporter's hunches alone, so it would be difficult to prove. He contacted his Press Secretary and ordered an immediate sanction on the Washington Post for printing the article. Second, he scheduled a meeting with CIA Director Prescott and Secretary of State Lee to discuss the Dr. David Phillips issue. He didn't care one way or the other about Condoleeza's opinion of her post. He considered her to be insignificant, and the general public knew nothing of her diminished authority. He was more concerned with the increased attention being brought of the reparations movement. He had to stop Dr. Phillips. He figured that if he severed the head of the movement, the body would eventually follow.

The American deficit was at $150 trillion and he had no intention of giving one cent to the descendents of African American slaves. He felt that the money could be spent on a more important cause, like his worldwide war on terrorism. He wanted to control the world's oil supply and snatch it from the grasp of the *towel heads*.

He would only be President for four years, eight with successful re-election. He had to secure his financial future and the billions in Arab oil money was his for the taking. A war on terrorism was the perfect political camouflage. Within three short years, he was going to have all of the Arab leaders eating out of the palm of his hand, and those that didn't eat were going to starve, simple as that.

President Burrows had a lot of work to do and little time to complete it. He came to the conclusion that there were too many tasks for one man to complete alone, even with his genius. He was going to have to delegate duties and utilize the people that he had beneath him. The power weapons of the CIA, FBI, and the American military were his toys to play with in his plot to rule the world. He felt a new sense of relief with his new approach. All he had to do was sit back, give orders, delegate duties, and criticize performance. He was going to use other people to do his dirt, and sit back and receive all the credit. He was going to use his power and position to have people work for him. For the first time in Cheney Burrows' life, he was going to see how it felt to be George Bush.

Doug Wingers was outraged with the Washington Post. They refused to purchase his latest article about scandal going on in the White House. It was an in-depth, personal interview with the parents of Jim Irvin, an Oklahoma man that had mysteriously disappeared. His parents talked about a George Bush look-alike contest. Jim had won first prize, $100,000 and a trip to Washington to meet the President. Nobody had heard from him since. Doug was faxed a picture of Jim and he had a remarkable likeness to former President Bush.

The sudden change of heart by the Washington Post made Doug fear that something was wrong. Maybe his instincts were true and the political bigwigs had made a few phone calls to shake things up. Doug had traveled too far and been through too much as a beat reporter to be easily intimidated. He didn't scare very easily and the Washington Post wasn't the only candy store in town. Doug had several contacts at many reputable newspapers, and even a few gossip tabloids. His story was not going to be silenced by President Burrows, or anyone else. He was going to make headlines and get to the bottom of this political scandal. He was going to figure out what really happened in the White House, no matter what it took. The powers that be were not going to scare him away that easy. Doug was a seasoned veteran in his field and had a reputation to uphold. He knew that he was on to something and he was very close to uncovering a major story. His reporter's instinct had never led him wrong in 20 years of journalism. If he were lucky enough to break the news of this story, he would be the envy of all his associates. It would make up for all the blunders of the past and probably lead to a promotion to editor of his newspaper. Too much was at risk for Doug Winters to pack up and leave Washington. He was so close to the truth that he could smell it, but he wanted more. He wanted the truth on a platter.

Dr. David Phillips had finally been granted a meeting with President Burrows. He sat in a leather chair, looking at the new President with the utmost confidence. He knew all about President Burrows and the slimy route he took to power as a yes man to George Bush. The dislike was mutual, but Dr. Phillips had made too much noise and now President Burrows was forced to meet with him face to face.

Dr. David Phillips had taken America by storm with his charismatic style and dashing good looks. He was the leader of the RNF, Reparations Now Forever, an African American nationalist organization that had chapters in every major city in America. He was a powerful speaker and had a devoted following, not just among African Americans, but he enjoyed international fame and recognition with powerful political support in England, France, Germany, Nigeria, China, Spain, and Japan. They all supported his self-help program and the reparations bill and the establishment of $1 trillion over a period of 100 years to establish satellite communities for African Americans to form a sovereign nation. In his view, African Americans had no true home. Their ancestors had been kidnapped from Africa and brought to this country against their will. He believed that America owed African Americans for the free labor and millions of people that died as a result of 400 years of slavery.

He wanted a separate but equal state for African Americans with its own political, economic and cultural identity. Of course, President Burrows thought Dr. David Phillips should have been thrown in an insane asylum, but this meeting was impossible to avoid.

"Greetings, Mr. President," Dr. Phillips said respectfully.

"Good afternoon, David. Congratulations on your Nobel Prize nomination," the President responded, especially careful not to use the term *Doctor* in reference to an African American man. Dr. Phillips had made headlines with his economic programs that led him to a nomination for the Nobel Prize.

"How's the wife?" A low blow. Everyone knew about the President's marital problems.

"What is your order of business? My time is valuable." Ignoring the insult, President Burrows wanted to move on. He couldn't stand the sight of such an arrogant African American man. He wanted to string him up from a tree.

"Well, as you know, the African American voters were promised a reparations bill by former President Bush. We supported his candidacy for the White House. He received our votes, he received our help. We just want you politicians to keep your promises."

"The bill has been discussed. I will get back to you. Anything else?" The President hoped for no response, but he knew Dr. Phillips better than that.

"Well, the RNF has over 20 million members in America and throughout the world. We plan to have a million people on the White House lawn each month until the bill is funded. I will go on every network, ABC, CBS, CNN PBS, BET, NBC, and reveal the lies that have been told by this administration. The world will know of our plight and I will not rest until this bill is passed." He got up without saying goodbye and walked out of the Oval Office.

President Burrows was fuming and could not believe that he was being threatened by someone whom he believed was beneath him. He was not going to let him get away with such blatant disrespect and getting the last word. He hadn't had a chance to throw him out of the Oval Office. Dr. Phillips had officially won their first battle, but there was an entire war left to fight. The President was already in the process of planning his counterattack. He had allowed the situation to go too far without giving his full attention. Now the RNF was out of control and had unbridled support in both the Senate and the House of Representatives. The reparations bill movement had to be stopped.

A million people on the White House lawn would be impossible to ignore. The media would have a field day and Dr. David Phillips was a master manipulator. He was as unpredictable as the weather and he had a very loyal following. Even President Burrows knew the extent of his power. When Dr. Phillips talked, everybody listened. He had to implement a plan that would shut him up forever.

Condoleeza could not believe her eyes when she returned to her home and found her husband, Bill, sitting on the sofa. He had conveniently let himself into her home. He knew Condoleeza all too well and her tendency to leave a spare key underneath the doormat. Bill knew a lot about human behavior patterns; the main reason why he was one of the top lawyers in the Chicago area. Bill missed his wife desperately and wanted to get to the bottom of her meteoric rise to fame in Washington. He wanted a piece of the action, or at least a few political big shots as referrals.

"What are you doing," Condoleeza said to a smiling Bill Kincaid.

"I was bored without you, hon," Bill replied in his best closing argument voice.

"How dare you come to my house unannounced? You know it's against the law to trespass. I'm the Vice President of the United States."

"My sentiments exactly. The Vice President of the United States should have more security than that. I could have been a burglar. What's really going on, Condoleeza?" Bill was brutally honest and straightforward, and he knew that she was hiding something.

"I don't want to talk about it. The nerve of you barging into my business. You have no respect for my feelings. I want you to leave now!"

Bill knew his limits and he had proved his point.

"I'm getting tired of this treatment. You're on your own. I'll start the divorce papers as soon as I get back to Chicago." Bill had pulled his final ace out of the hole.

"Fine, do what you have to do," Condoleeza said, almost in relief. A burden was successfully off her shoulders. "Where is my spare key?"

Bill tossed it to her and said, "You're going to need me before I need you." He left without any further comments. Those damn lawyers, they loved making dramatic exits.

Condoleeza was alone again and hoped that she had made the right decision. It was strange that Bill had just dropped by out of the blue. It was not like him to act insecure or check up on her. She could never go back to Chicago now. Everyone would look at her as a failure. Regardless of how watered down her position as Vice President was, she made up her mind to stay. She was a survivor. She approached her position with a new sense of urgency. Her marriage was officially over and now all she had left was her pride. Nothing or nobody was going to take that away from her. She had gone through too much to get this far.

Eugene L. Weems, Timothy R. Richardson

CHAPTER 8

Another routine meeting for the Sons of Liberty at the Oval Office. President Burrows, Secretary of State Lee, Admiral Striker, and CIA Director Prescott are all present.

"David Lee Phillips is a problem. He must be dealt with," said a worried President Burrows.

"We have options. We can perform the normal character assassination or we can terminate him altogether," Prescott offered.

"We can't involve the military. It's a domestic matter," the Admiral added.

"We have an informant very close to him and the subject is a clear and present danger to our cause," Prescott explained in detail.

"Let's terminate the bastard," an agitated Secretary of State interjected.

President Burrows explained that there could be major fallout and that David Phillips had over 20 million devoted followers.

91

"We have the strongest military forces in the world," the admiral added, not to be intimidated.

"Okay, fine. Prescott, I want him terminated," the President said.

"It's a done deal," Prescott said with a sly smile.

Another day had come to pass for President Burrows and his lovely wife, Mary Ann. After a brief sexual encounter, the two engaged in pillow talk. Mary Ann had a mastery over Cheney's fragile psyche. He shared everything with her. Through their relationship, he would try to make up for what he lacked in sexual prowess by sharing juicy political secrets. He would impress her with political moves before they were made public. He told her about George's disappearance, the token appointment of Condoleeza Kincaid, and even about the inner dealings of the Ku Klux Klan. Mary Ann knew the identities of many of the high-ranking officials underneath the white sheets and marveled at how they functioned undetected in everyday society. Now that she had the most powerful husband in the country, the secrets flowed like a waterfall. Almost every night, Cheney would rave about the Sons of Liberty and how powerful he was. Mary Ann would stroke his ego until she got every ounce of information from him. No secret could be kept away from Mrs. Burrows, not even the plot to kill Dr. David Phillips.

Cheney was never concerned about what he told Mary Ann. It was just his naïve attempt to add spice to his relationship. A major void was created when he no longer had George Bush as an information source. He loved to use his dazzling intellect to keep his lover satisfied. He loved to have her beg for information and torment herself mentally trying to figure things out. He couldn't physically satisfy her in bed, but he had mastered the art of a great brain fuck. It was the only time when he was in control of their relationship and the only reason that Mary Ann continued to put up with him.

Despite all of his genius and superior sophistication, Cheney could not resist the temptation to indulge in self-adulation. The gossip was as good as ever these days. He had an entire nation at his disposal and controlled the intelligence-gathering agencies of America. He was a walking encyclopedia of top secrets and would not hesitate to create a scandal or two if he lacked something to talk about. His ego was out of control. It was too much power for one man to have.

Mary Ann marveled at the level her husband had stooped in order to gain such power. She was the undisputed star of the beauty salon's weekly gossip sessions. All the wives of the political big shots would gather and brag about the exploits of their husbands. The show could not begin without a grand entrance by the First Lady. She was the envy of all the women at Norma's. Mary Ann predicted front page news as if she were Cleo the Psychic. Nobody knew as much as the reigning queen of Washington D.C. Her gossip sessions had reached the point of euphoria.

Norma's small boutique had reached a record level of popularity. Everybody who was anybody went to her salon for inside information. Mary Ann Wednesdays was the new talk of the town. The gossip would begin there and then each woman would leave with their versions of the news and take it to their individual circles. Before you knew it, all of Washington D.C. knew the intimate secrets of the White House. Mary Ann didn't mind that she spread highly sensitive information that threatened American national security because she was the center of attention. President Burrows was unaware that the biggest terrorist in his war against terrorism shared the bed with him at the White House. With all of his power and infinite knowledge, the President failed to realize that his wife was leaking secrets from the White House like a dripping water faucet.

"John Doe, Cell 12," the intercom sounded off loudly in C holding tank. A bewildered George Bush awoke inside his Acirema cell. He was met by two big, black prison guards who were strictly business. The two men guided him through the maze of hallways and corridors to an immaculate office. A bald, older black man sat behind a large desk. He had three gold bars on his collar and several awards decorated the walls of his office. As he was unhandcuffed and sat down in front of the imposing figure, George knew immediately that something was wrong. He knew power when he saw it. George had met with some of the most powerful men in the world.

"I'm Commander King, Prison Superintendent," the man said, as if he had said it a million times in the mirror. For the first time in his life, George was outclassed and felt intimidated.

"I'm...I'm George Bush from --"

"The United States," the commander finished his statement.

George sat there with his mouth open as if he had seen a ghost. How did Commander King know about the United States? It was only information that he had shared with his white allies in secret prison circles.

"I know all about you and the trouble you have caused in my prison," an informed Commander King stated. The intimidation that George felt was at an all-time high. He sat there speechless, like a child in the principal's office. No words could save him from his predetermined fate, so he sat there and hoped for leniency.

"You should be more careful. I have ears all over this facility," the superintendent said in a confidence-filled voice. Still silent, the former messiah was at a loss for words.

"Twenty-one days in the hole. Remove this maggot from my sight!"

Commander King was heartless and George was stunned. George was escorted from the office by the two uniformed officers. They led him deep into the bowels of the prison through several corridors, to a dark part of nothingness that held a stench beyond belief. He held his breath and could not believe that humans were capable of living in such an environment. It was as unsanitary as the worst kept zoo. The horrid stench reeked of a witchy brew of urine and shit. He had never visualized a place so unpleasant, not even in his worst nightmare. If Acirema was hell, this place was officially hell's basement.

George closed his eyes and tried desperately to visualize his life as it once existed in the luxuries of his Texas estate. He sought a visual escape from his reality. He hoped that he would open his eyes and it would all be an unwelcome fantasy, a long, horrible and pain-filled nightmare for all of his past sins. If he ever doubted the existence of God, now he realized that he was terribly wrong. He prayed in silence and hoped for an instant relief, divine intervention, or an unannounced miracle. Prison life had already been a horrible experience, but he feared that the worst was yet to come. Where did he make his mistake? How had his life gone so horribly wrong? Who did he offend? He gave a failed attempt at struggling in efforts to prevent his fate. Eventually, he was tossed into a small, dark cell the size of a large casket, and then there was silence.

The front page of the Washington Post read, *Vice President Condoleeza Kincaid Files for Divorce*. It was a public relations nightmare for an already shaky White House reputation. President Burrows cursed himself. "Shit, I should have fired that nigger bitch a long time ago." He could not believe that she had brought so much negative attention to his political campaign. He felt that he should have followed the advice of his associate in the south and passed her over for the Vice President position. He viewed it as too much authority for an ape to handle, but he thought that even Condoleeza Kincaid could handle the watered down version of the position. His instincts had proven wrong and he had not paid enough attention to her CIA report to see this situation coming. He had to do something, so he called CIA Director Prescott on the red line. After a few rings, the director answered.

"Yes, Mr. President?"

"The Condoleeza Kincaid situation is out of control. I want the media silenced. Put an agent on her full time. Make sure he's black and handsome, if that's at all possible," the President ordered as a possible solution.

"I have the perfect man for the job, Agent Timothy Richardson," the CIA director responded after probing his memory.

"Whoever, I don't care. We can't afford to have this whore continue to embarrass us. I will shoot her myself if necessary." The President was angry beyond belief.

Prescott replied, "I will handle it, sir."

"Then do it now!" The two angry men hung up at the same time.

Timothy Richardson was a stunning presence of a man. He was the product of a mixed relationship, an African American father and Italian mother. Growing up, he had all the best of both worlds and his features were *GQ* cover material. He had attended one of the best schools on a college football scholarship, the University of Nevada, Las Vegas. He was a decent football athlete who had played a few years in the NFL but was not Hall of Fame material. Timothy could not settle for being average. He wanted more out of life. After football, he entered the Las Vegas drug trade and had become one of the biggest dope dealers in West Nevada. He was handsome, football tough, and well-respected. His reputation was eventually known all over the country. Casanova is what they called him.

In no time at all, his reputation became a little too well-known and the federal alphabet soup agencies were on to him. The FBI, CIA, and DEA all had files and Prescott won the contest and captured the biggest fish. The arrest made national headlines and the Las Vegas Casanova had achieved his moment in the sun. He went into the Hall of Fame with the most notorious drug lords. The money, material possessions, and power was unmatched. He had over half the cheerleaders in the NFL on his payroll and clients from coast to coast. Everyone knew about him, men envied him, and women wanted to fuck him. It all came to an end at the hands of a young Agent Prescott, but to everyone's astonishment, Timothy cooperated. He cut a deal and told the CIA everything. He gave up all of his celebrity clients and his Columbian connections. The CIA and DEA combined for one of the biggest international drug raids in history. Over $500 million and 13,000 kilos of cocaine were confiscated. The raid was all the leverage Agent Prescott needed for his resume. He went to the number one spot of the CIA brass with a bullet and was appointed director when Bill Boyer retired. The rest was history.

Director Prescott owed it all to Timothy Richardson, the 'big fish' that made his career. He eventually got him a pardon from prison because of security concerns for his safety. Finally, Prescott had convinced the political powers that be that Timothy would be a better service to his country as a member of the CIA instead of rotting in a prison cell. He won the argument and Agent Timothy Richardson was born, and had been one of his top agents ever since that day. He was still a lady's man and nobody could match his style. He was the perfect remedy to the Condoleeza Kincaid situation. How do you handle a high-priced whore? Introduce her to a wealthy pimp.

Dr. David Phillips had just finished a heart-wrenching speech to an ocean of adoring followers. It was the first speech in his promised Million a Month campaign for reparations. The White House lawn will never be the same. History had been made for the cause. It was also one of the noisiest rallies ever held on American soil. He was at the prime of his career and had never been so popular and influential in all of his days. He was a winner of the Nobel Prize for economics, had brought the African American call for reparations to the floor of the United States, and the world was now his audience. People had labeled him the next coming of

Malcolm X with the charisma of Dr. Martin Luther King, Jr. His image was recognized throughout the world and people loved him. Dr. Phillips was a lively legend.

He shook the hands of all who approached him, one by one. If it were up to him, he would shake each of his supporters' hands one by one. Over a million people would gladly kiss his feet for an opportunity to meet him. Security was as tight as a Mariah Carey dress and he was virtually surrounded by bodyguards.

As he continued his post speech ritual, a sharply dressed white man approached him to shake his hand. Dr. Phillips reached out and acknowledged the hand placed in front of him. "Ouch," the doctor yelped, as a sharp object, like a sewing needle, pierced the flesh of his hand. He snatched his hand away from the stranger and winced in pain. In a matter of seconds, security was upon the culprit and he was ushered away. A funny sensation overcame Dr. Phillips, but he just shook it off and continued his ritual of shaking hands with everyone who approached him. Three days later, Dr. David Lee Phillips collapsed in his Beverly Hills mansion from a heart attack.

Condoleeza Kincaid was in court in Chicago and was the first Vice President of the United States in history to go through a divorce. It was another first to add to her ever growing list of accomplishments. Bill had pulled some strings and expedited the divorce proceedings. He also made public his intentions of writing a tell-all autobiography and already had a bidding war going on between several of the top publishers for exclusive publishing rights. He made his divorce from the Vice President as public as possible and the courtroom was a media circus.

Condoleeza's life was crumbling before her eyes. Bill had made public every intimate detail of their relationship and things were ugly. He had pictures of her torrid affair with the escort in Washington D.C., recorded phone conversations, receipts for every item he had purchased for her, and even had every single time they had sex documented to the day and hour. He was out to ruin her life. President Burrows had met with her and demanded that she resign from her post, but she refused to sign the paperwork. She was not about to voluntarily leave her only source of income. She was going to force him to fire her, that way she could at least get unemployment benefits.

It seemed like everything was going wrong. Her divorce looked bad, her job was meaningless, and she was going to lose large amounts of money in court to Bill. The only positive thing in her life was when she met Agent Timothy Richardson, her personal bodyguard. He had been there for her every step of the way.

Condoleeza confided in Agent Richardson and shared so much with him. In such a short period of time, it was safe to say that Condoleeza trusted in him. They had been through so much together since he had been appointed as her personal bodyguard. There was a lot for her to like about Agent Richardson. He was handsome, intelligent, and strong. She had no problems with the probing mob of reporters that followed her like bees would follow honey. Timothy protected her like a caring and compassionate father. His strength was a welcome breath of fresh air.

Condoleeza was at a period in her life where she was very vulnerable and she needed a strong shoulder to lean on for support. Agent Richardson provided that strong shoulder in time of need. His relationship with her had become more than professional. She had feelings for him that were more than a high school crush. To top things off, Condoleeza was now going to be very single and could not afford to get caught parading around the single social scene in Washington. President Burrows had already warned her that one more mishap would cost her dearly and that he wouldn't hesitate to have her terminated. Too much negative attention was already on the White House and he was not going to jeopardize getting impeached for her.

Her physical need for sexual gratification was growing constantly. It had grown into an itch that would have to be scratched. She had the perfect candidate at her beck and call. She was already looking him up and down like eye candy. She wondered how big his dick was. He had big feet. Anything would be an improvement over the five inches that Bill tickled her with. Timothy was a gift to her from God. Nobody would question her relationship with him because he was her bodyguard. After the death of Dr. Phillips, she didn't want to take any chances trying to meet anyone new.

Besides, she had not slept with a black man since high school and it was the perfect way to get even with Bill.

Her ex-husband had almost ruined her. The divorce was a total disaster. She regretted marrying a lawyer. He had too many connections at City Hall. He got half of all her assets and even got the mansion in Chicago. She thanked God for Bill's low sperm count and the fact that they couldn't have kids. Actually, Condoleeza was relieved that the divorce was finally over. She had won in the relationship and got what she wanted, fame, popularity, and she was the Vice President of the United States of America. She no longer needed her white *boy toy* to carry around with her. She enjoyed her independence, and besides Oprah, she wasn't married. It was time for her to sow her royal oats and Agent Timothy Richardson looked as good as a breakfast bowl of oatmeal.

On the day that Dr. Phillips was announced dead, several major riots erupted throughout the country. President Burrows had to declare martial law on Los Angeles, Compton, New York, Detroit, Harlem, Dallas, Philadelphia, Chicago, St. Louis, New Orleans, Houston, and Cleveland. Major cities were going up in smoke. Blacks rioted all over the world. President Burrows could not believe the response he received from the American public. As soon as Dr. Phillips died, everyone blamed the American government for foul play. Prior to his death, Dr. Phillips made public that he and President

Burrows were enemies. Many of his followers knew about the CIA needle and Dr. Phillips had all of the symptoms. He was in perfectly good health and jogged five miles a day. He had even discussed the incident that occurred at the Million a Month rally with the upper brass of the RNF.

The funeral was magnificent. It was a funeral befitting a king. The Sons of Liberty's plan had backfired. They had made Dr. Phillips an eternal living martyr. Leaders from around the world, entertainers, politicians, musicians, kings, queens, professional athletes, doctors, lawyers, and commoners all came to pay their last respects to Dr. Phillips. There were millions of people at the wake. It made the death of Pope John Paul II look like a crowd at a Milli Vanilly reunion concert. The entire nation was shut down for a week. Everyone that was anybody was in Chicago.

President Burrows was urged not to attend due to threats on his life from the RNF. Several African American members of the Army, Navy, Air Force, Marines, CIA, and FBI defected and joined the RNF. It was almost a modern day revolution. The Sons of Liberty had started a war. Worldwide attention was brought to the cause for African Americans receiving reparations from the American government. The RNF could not have paid money for the publicity that they received.

To make matters worse, the RNF had proven to be far more organized than the Sons of Liberty had anticipated. Eugene Weems was immediately appointed President.

He was an extreme radical and made Dr. Phillips look like a Winnie the Pooh. He was an African American militant that believed in an eye for an eye. His checkered background as a Navy Seal more than made him a threat. He was very aware of the chaos that America caused throughout the world using the disguise of a war on terrorism. He urged African Americans in America to buy guns and organize in their communities. He did not believe in politics. Eugene Weems was a man of action. The death of Dr. Phillips did not destroy a movement, it had awakened a sleeping giant.

Eugene L. Weems, Timothy R. Richardson

CHAPTER 9

Mary Ann Burrows was sitting at the beauty salon addressing her audience with juicy gossip about the events going on at the White House. She was on a roll and had even predicted Condoleeza being appointed Vice President of the United States. Word had spread around town that Mary Ann was psychic. She could predict the outcome of political events before they happened. Mary Ann loved the attention and she had a loyal following. There were so many people in the beauty salon that she did not notice a new face in the crowd. Surprisingly, it was a male and the last thing on his mind was patronizing Norma's beauty salon. Doug Winters was interested in the gossip because gossip made the best stories.

"I don't know why those people are so crazy about that Dr. Phillips. They should have known he wasn't going to last long after getting smart with my Cheney. Now they are never going to get their money. How do they expect us to give them money? We didn't have anything to do with slavery. I told you that he was going to end up dead." Mary Ann spoke with the confidence of a seasoned politician. The salon was silent as she made her announcement. "The CIA did it."

Armed with enough ammunition, Doug bolted from his seat and made his exit. He was on his article to life. All of the media outlets in the Washington area were afraid to do business with him for fear of government sanctions. President Burrows had too much power over local media sources and already labeled Doug as a terrorist threat. His article about Jim Irvin almost got him thrown in jail and he was not about to play ball on the President's home turf anymore. He knew that Condoleeza Kincaid was still in Chicago finalizing her divorce proceedings. He had to figure out a way to meet with her. She was a fellow journalist and he thought about using that common experience as an angle.

He was running out of options and he knew that the CIA was on to him. He had to let things cool off a bit. He was a dummy, but he was no fool. Even he realized when he was outmanned. He would have to plan his attack in secret and lay low for a while. No time was better than the present because there were enough distractions with the turmoil surrounding Dr. Phillips' death. Doug was not about to give up because he only knew one way to live, and that was on the edge. He had been in trouble before and he knew that the only way to get back in the media game was to deliver a breaking story. After hearing the juicy details from Mary Ann, his pen was already working overtime.

George Bush was strictly skin and bones as he struggled to refocus his eyes to light. It had been over three weeks in the hole, and a life of bread and water. He had a new attitude and had never been through a more difficult struggle. He almost died in the hole, but what didn't kill him only could make him stronger. He deeply wanted his nightmare to end and for whatever Gods that be to have mercy on his soul. He did a lot of thinking while he was in the hole and he was more determined than ever to escape. He was not about to spend the rest of his life in prison.

As George continued his journey back to his prison cell, he looked for any weakness in the security system. He was beyond the point of desperation and would have sold his soul to get back to his life of luxury in America. He was escorted back to the confines of his cell and found that he had a new cellmate.

"Hey, I'm John," the stranger said, introducing himself.

"What happened to Ken," a weak and frustrated George muttered in response to the greeting.

"He rolled it up and went home, lucky son of a bitch," John replied.

George knew that Ken had two more years left on his sentence and an early release only could mean one thing, Ken was the person that snitched him out. George had never been to prison before, but he was receiving a crash course on prison ethics. The fact of the matter was that there was no honor among thieves and every man was for himself. The entire time, Ken had served as a voice recorder for the prison warden. Now an additional ten years was added to his prison term and he lost all of his good time. His back was further against the wall at the expense of a careless mistake.

In prison, mistakes cost you dearly and more time was something George could not afford to lose. He didn't know how he was going to get back to America, but he knew that he could not get there from his prison cell. The route back to the White House was somewhere in the Black House of President Barack Obama. Somehow, George had to find his way back there and find it. He knew that he couldn't make it on his own, but he could not trust anyone. He was stuck between a rock and a hard place.

The fact of the matter was clear and he was not about to make the same mistake twice. He looked John over like a cheap suit and assumed that he was another political parrot for Warden King. He was going to have to make moves in secrecy and screen his allies like potential employees. Another bid in the hole would turn out to be a fate worse than being buried alive. Time almost stood still in prison. The minutes went by like hours and the hours passed by like days. It was time to build another plan. George was as determined as ever to change his predicament and prayed for a little good luck. The cynical thoughts began to brew around in his mind like coffee. He was not going to give up. A quitter never wins and a winner never quits. He had made up his mind. He had over three billion reasons to continue his struggle. He was not about to quit.

President Burrows met with CIA Director Prescott in the Oval Office. The entire country had almost gone up in flames before his spectacled eyes. His approval rating was at an all-time low and rumors circulated that he was the worst President the country had ever seen. The economy was horrible, foreign relations suffered, and government spending went through the roof. He was being blamed for the death of Dr. David Lee Phillips and the Million a Month Rally was now the Two Million a Month Rally. Eugene Weems and his supporters camped out on the White House lawn like squatters. He almost regretted having Dr. Phillips terminated. The new leader of the RNF had more security than the pope. Even the government had trouble finding a way to implant an infiltrator.

It was a struggle, but he finally had regained control of the country. He was grateful for the National Guard and the Armed Services. Even with the many defections, America was still a dominant world power. The only thing that prevented a revolt was his continued public support of Condoleeza, despite her divorce. He was happy that he had listened to Prescott and kept at least one token black around in his administration.

Too much attention had been brought to the movement for reparations and the entire world threatened sanctions against America. He feared embargos from

China, Africa, and Japan. The list was growing longer by the day. They demanded that America pay all of its bills. He did not want his country to meet the same fate of a post cold war Russia.

The President plotted his next course of action like an experienced navigator. "Director Prescott, have we infiltrated the RNF yet," he asked his partner in crime.

"We had one operative initiated into the organization, but he was discovered and swiftly terminated. Weems runs a tighter ship than the Mayflower," Prescott responded.

"Well, you will find a way in. Nobody can have that much power. Out of 20 million followers, somebody has to have a price," the President replied, almost sounding like his old friend, George Bush.

"I have several men on it. We've lost ten agents already. The problem is getting past his elite security force, the Black Sphinx."

"I don't care about a fucking black sphinx or a black anything. I want results. We spend billions on homeland security and I want heads to roll."

"Mr. President, this Eugene Weems is a highly intelligent former Navy Seal Commander and was highly decorated. He fought in two wars and --"

"Shut up, Prescott. We are the American government and we create wars for a hobby! I want this nigger infiltrated and I want them off my fucking front lawn; is that understood?" The President drove his point home by slamming his fist on his desk.

"It's a done deal." Prescott left the Oval Office with a big chunk chewed out of his already flat ass.

President Burrows sat at his desk like a Napoleonic dictator. He contemplated his next move like a skilled surgeon. Tiny beads of sweat formed on his forehead and he was steaming mad; Robin was doing a horrible job as Batman. George had made being a superhero look so easy. He had to do something and he had to do it fast. The RNF had become a major distraction that had his attention. He remembered one thing from his good friend, George, and it was, *Never let them see you sweat*. President Burrows reached in the chest pocket of his designer blazer to grab a handkerchief, because the heat was on and he was sweating.

Doug Winters had made it back to Chicago in record time. He was happy to be on his home turf and far away from the politics that ran him out of Washington. After pleading and begging, he had finally made amends with Carl Watson and got his job back at the *Chicago Tribune*. His articles on Cheney Burrows had sold too many newspapers and made too much money for him to be turned away forever. The same idiot that had cost him his job was his meal ticket with the newspaper. He had to be more careful before making any more attempts at branching out. A hunch was not good enough anymore. He would only make moves based on actual facts. He had to lay low for a while and brew his story about the Dr. Philips assassination to perfection. The entire nation was still in an uproar and there were people waiting impatiently for any opportunity to get revenge.

He already had the powers that be at the White House in an uproar behind his article on President Bush. If only he could back up his accusations with the facts of the President's whereabouts. He was still missing like Elvis. If Jim Irvin was the real person who died in the explosion, where was the real President? Why was Cheney Burrows still supporting Condoleeza Kincaid? Who were the Sons of Liberty? Who killed Dr. Phillips, and why?

So many questions lingered that needed to be answered. Doug knew that he was on the right track because there were too many government sources in Washington trying to silence him. In all his years of working in the field of journalism, he'd learned that comfort was a journalist's worst enemy. Any time a journalist felt comfortable about pursuing a story, it wasn't a world changer. Doug was into charging the world. He wanted to be remembered forever.

Doug had a hot lead, but he was back to square one. He had to get to Condoleeza before she went back to Washington D.C. He also had to go to the coroner's office and do a little research on Dr. Phillips' autopsy report. A heart attack seemed too simple of a death. He realized that it was a gamble working on a conspiracy theory that pointed a finger at the United States Government. It was a risk that he was prepared to take. He knew that the government powers that be were on to him, and the same government agencies that killed Dr.

Phillips could make him a distant memory in a heartbeat. Doug liked living, but he loved a breaking news story better than sex. He was going to get to the bottom of what was going on at any cost. A good news story was well worth the struggle, but a world-changing story was worth dying for.

Condoleeza had paid her respects to Dr. Phillips, but she did not like the reception she received from the RNF as the first African American Vice President of the United States. The new RNF leader, Eugene Weems, did not even recognize her presence. She heard the mumblings of the words *sell out, Aunt Jemima*, and *Oreo* used in reference to her. She felt as uncomfortable as a hooker in church on Easter Sunday. It really disturbed her not to be recognized and accepted by her own people. She felt like an unwelcome outsider. It was a shame, because as a politician she supported Dr. Phillips' reparations movement. It was sad that nobody ever asked her how she felt about the movement. Everyone assumed that she was a politician being controlled by President Burrows.

Well, it wasn't the first time that Condoleeza felt like an outsider. She thanked God for Agent Richardson for the hundredth time. He was a panty-soaking breath of fresh air. She had surpassed the point of infatuation with him. By now, she was ready to taste him. She had flirted with him long enough. It was time to cash in on her advances. He had been so supportive over the past few months and a sexual attraction had developed for a black man for the first time since she was in high school. She felt so strong and protected whenever Timothy was around. It was a great feeling and she enjoyed the time that they spent alone in her apartment. Vice President Kincaid already had her mind made up, it was about time for her to get back in touch with her roots.

Eugene Weems had a newfound motivation to enter into the political world. He hated politics with a passion, but he was not going to let that get in the way of avenging his best friend's death. Dr. Phillips passed the torch to him on his deathbed and the flames were still burning as bright as ever. He was not going to let the memory of his old friend die. They had been through too much together, starting the movement for reparations in Dr. Phillips' basement. David played the no-nonsense problem solver in the shadows. He was the security advisor and Dr. Phillips' closest ally, and now he was the hand-picked leader chosen to lead the RNF.

Eugene moved in silence, mostly at night. He had no family or relatives that anyone knew of. No wife, no children, no brothers and no sisters, not even a pet. His background was a mystery and Dr. Phillips was the only person who knew about his parents. Rumor had it that he was an alien from the twelfth planet. Mr. Weems was as mysterious as the pyramids of Garza. The only thing that was publicly known about him was his commitment to his people and his devotion to the reparations movement. He was a dedicated warrior for the cause.

Dr. Phillips had explained his conspiracy theory to him in total secrecy. He had told him all about the handshake that began his demise and the dreaded CIA needle. Eugene was going to be more careful. His best friend had fallen at the hands of the government and he could not trust anyone. Every bit of Navy Seal training he had learned in the academy was going to be necessary to accomplish his goal. He had a bone to pick with President Burrows and he hated him just as much as Burrows hated African American people. His White House informant had told him all about the secret meetings of the so-called Sons of Liberty. He had developed his own security organization from the ranks of the RNF, the Black Sphinx. His militant branch of the RNF was worldwide and had members themselves, but everybody knew one thing; the Black Sphinx could make you disappear.

Laura Bush had bought and settled into a new mansion in Georgia with her two nearly adorable children. A metamorphosis had taken place. She was a responsible parent for the first time in her life. She was still relatively popular in the State of Georgia. Without George to boss her around, she did not know what to do. It started off as a joke she shared with her parents over apple pie, but eventually she decided to take a chance and run for Senator of Georgia. She was still young, smart, and a billionaire heiress. The Bush name still had a strong public following in the South. Laura figured that she could do well in the world of politics. She was great at telling people what to do and she had played a big part in getting her husband elected President.

The world was going to be introduced to a new Laura Bush; independent, strong and decisive. She had hired Tony Gibson, Willa Mae's son, as her personal bodyguard. He was a black man, but somehow he had earned Laura's trust. She had begun to confide in him and Jenna looked up to him as an authority figure. It had been so long since Laura had felt the comforts of a positive man, and Tony filled that void. If a person didn't know her, one would think that she was becoming attracted to him. She caught herself fantasizing about running her fingers over his strong, black body and once caught herself gazing at his crotch. She wondered how big his penis was and how it would feel inside of her. Her vagina was in dire need of attention. Anything would have been an improvement over Bush. He was so arrogant that he kept a written record of how many times they had engaged in sex. She had lived a sheltered life and was curious about the rumored sexual prowess of black men. Laura knew that it was an experience that was just waiting to happen. The two of them spent too much time alone together and the uncomfortable stares between them only added fuel to the fire. Tony was shy, so Laura was going to have to make the first move.

Her life post-George was really looking up. She had purchased a new mansion in Atlanta, her children were following her rules, she had a promising political career ahead of her, and she was still worth boat loads of money. The only thing missing from her life was romance and she was about to kick things off with Tony. She was so happy to be out of Washington and closer to home. A seat on the Senate was going to be the final cherry on top. She figured that if George could fool the world and make people think enough of his fortune to elect him President of the United States, that they would think at least half as much for her and elect her as a senator from Georgia. She was still drop-dead gorgeous and had several connections in the state. She viewed it as a beauty pageant kicked up a higher level. She had to do a lot of politicizing to get elected Miss America and was willing to do the same for her seat in the Senate. Laura was used to getting what she wanted and was not about to change one bit.

George had considerably cut back on his talks about a country named the United States of America. As a matter of fact, he hardly said anything to anybody. He actually kept his thoughts to himself for the first time in his life. It was a complete turnaround from the charismatic charmer that had deceived an entire country into voting him President of the United States. His cellmate, John, was far different from Ken. He was just as quiet as George and had the personality of a door knob. It was going to be a long time spent in prison for

George and his communication skills were going to probably regress to the days of the cave man.

Late at night, he would lay on his bunk and have memories of his life back in America. He missed being a billionaire and having control over thousands of people. He missed telling his beautiful wife what to do and being the head of his household. He would think about how perfect his life used to be and he would cry tears of sadness. It was killing him deep inside and he longed to return to America and his life as a billionaire. He would have given his soul in return for a night's rest in his Texas estate. George had to figure out a plan, a way to get out of the hell hole that he was living in. He didn't mind risking another trip to the hole. It was obvious to him that eventually he was going to have to trust in somebody.

"Hey, John, my name is George Bush. I'm from a country called the United States." George finally broke the silence. He was back in business.

President Burrows had finally overcome the chaos of the riots in almost every major city of America. Martial law had worked in regaining order to his country. Several months had passed and he finally had an informant in the RNF, Danny Sharpe. The One million a Month Rally was still a problem, but not even the powers of the President were enough to stop First Amendment rights. The rallies had toned down a bit, but Eugene Weems still had a loyal following. Cheney's war on terrorism gave him the opportunity to be gone from the White House for months at a time. He spent a lot of time at Camp David and other secret Presidential retreats.

The new Air Force One was always in the air. He thanked the devil for the diversion of terrorism against America and could not believe that America had fallen for it. It was his green light to a vacation any time he wished. Nobody would question the whereabouts of the President during a time of war. He had to stir up more trouble with the nations of the world. He needed another smoke screen to hide behind. It had been over a year since he had taken office and he had not performed one meaningful Presidential duty. His only claim to fame was his war on terrorism. He had some cleaning up to do. He had to silence Doug Winters forever and stop the millions of people that crowded the White House lawn every month, two factors that were the only things standing between him and a successful re-election. The American public would never vote a new face into the White House with a war still looming in the shadows. President Burrows started the war and he was the only person who was going to be trusted to stop it.

CHAPTER 10

Meanwhile, in Chicago, Doug Winters was putting the finishing touches on his article about his conspiracy theory on the death of Dr. Phillips. He had successfully done his research this time and had covered all angles. He had even included a few facts in his articles. He wrote about Norma's hair salon and Mary Ann Wednesdays. He had also done extensive research on the so-called CIA needle. He had more than enough ammunition to get his article in the Opinion section of the *Chicago Tribune*. His Editor in Chief would even take the risk of printing it in that section, and the paper could always write him off as a freelance lunatic reporter with an insane conspiracy theory. It was the only way to have his voice heard and he had to accept it.

A couple months had passed by since Dr. Phillips' funeral and racial tensions had subsided. However, the memory of Dr. Phillips' death was still fresh in the minds of his followers. Printing an article about his death would still be like putting salt in an open wound, but that was the chance that Doug would have to take. He had to print the truth. His career was in jeopardy. Journalism was the only life that he knew, and controversy was what paid his bills. If all else failed, he still had the interview to do with Vice President Condoleeza Kincaid. He still had the option of the tabloid circuit in the Chicago area, but that was a last resort. He had to make the most of his article in the *Chicago Tribune*. It may turn out to be his last.

Vice President Kincaid lay sleeping in the bed of her Chicago mansion, nude and sexually satisfied. Sex with Timothy had turned out to be a living fantasy beyond her wildest dream. He touched parts in the depths of her vagina that she never knew existed. She also discovered the sensation of multiple orgasms for the very first time. It was an earth shattering experience, far more than she had bargained for. It was great for Timothy, too. At first, he thought of it as another meaningless CIA assignment or another notch in his belt, but Condoleeza was different. She was smart, beautiful, and the Vice President of the United States. Timothy had already thrown everything that Director Prescott had told him about her out the window. He had developed his own image of how Condoleeza was and he liked what he saw.

"Wow, you truly are a special agent. I have never came like that before," Condoleeza confessed.

"I do my best to please, Ms. Vice President," Timothy responded.

"I must confess, the first time I caught you staring at me, it made me wet. Now I see why," Condoleeza said in a matter-of-fact tone.

"I think you are a beautiful and sexy woman. I love your eyes. It's as if I can see your soul." Timothy paid her the ultimate compliment.

"Do you like what you see," Condoleeza questioned.

"I must admit, I really like what I see," Timothy said, looking at Condoleeza seductively. Condoleeza was ready for round seven, as she rolled over in one fluid motion and was on top of Timothy, straddling him with passion in her eyes.

"Now you see what you've done? Every time we're alone you're going to have to make love to me like that, you understand." Condoleeza made her demand sound like a request.

"Your wish is my command, Ms. Vice President. It's my duty to serve my country."

The two love birds engaged in more sexual acts. Condoleeza had waited far too long for sexual gratification. It had been ages since she had been laid. So much tension was built up inside of her. It felt good to be wanted and she had the perfect *boy toy* in Timothy Richardson. He worked for her and was at her beck and call. It felt good to finally have somebody that respected her authority as Vice President. As she braced herself for another earth shattering climax, after taking orders and being at the bottom of the political totem pole for so long, it felt good for her to finally be on top.

Eugene Weems had just been briefed by his Minister of Security, Roberto Akbar. He was made aware of the CIA informant, Danny Sharpe, among the ranks of the RNF. To make matters worse, Mr. Weems had pledged him into the organization himself. He hated making any mistakes that made him look human, he was a perfectionist. It was a situation that he had to take care of with swiftness. He was going to make an example out of Agent Sharpe and for any other sellout that thought about infiltrating the RNF.

"Mr. Akbar, you are dismissed. Thanks for the one up." Roberto gave a salute and was acknowledged by the leader of the RNF. He then left the office and disappeared into the darkness. Eugene pulled out his cell phone and thumbed-in a discrete phone number. After one ring, it was answered.

"Yes, Mr. Weems." It was Peaches, a tall, leggy, young version of Pam Grier in the 1970s.

"I want you to handle things, Danny Eprahs, ASAP." He talked in a code only the Black Sphinx could understand.

"It's done, sir," Peaches said in response.

"Aye, peace out." He pressed the call end button on his closed circuit radio and lit a fine African cigar. He knew that things were in safe hands with Peaches on the job. He had trained her himself. Eugene Weems was already planning his counter attack. The powers that be at the White house were going to pay for this one. They were going to learn to respect his mind.

Two days later, Agent Sharpe was relaxing in the confines of a Jacuzzi at the Embassy Suites. It was a dream come true and he had just had the best sex of his life. He had finally nabbed Amira Shakur. It turned out to be another one of the many fringes of accepting the assignment to infiltrate the RNF. It was his dream assignment; drugs, money, and now the ultimate sex. He was almost ready for round two as Peaches blow dried her afro.

"When are you going to join me, baby? The water is getting cold," he said, almost relaxed.

"Well, I have a present for you from Eugene Weems." Agent Sharpe looked up just in time to see Peaches throw the blow dryer into the Jacuzzi. The electrical current shocked the life out of Agent Sharpe's body.

"Is that hot enough for ya," an accomplished Peaches said, as she grabbed her belongings and exited the hotel room. Danny boy was no more.

George Bush was finally warming up to John Rodgers after a turbulent courtship as cellmates. John had successfully broken the ice by sharing his commissary items with an indigent George. He was the only person that was nice to him in Acirema. Even George knew that eventually he was going to have to trust somebody.

"They say that you are a terrorist, too, a mad scientist," Bush inquired to John.

"Well, I am a scientist, and yes, my theory about Acirema being a twelfth planet to another solar system has been met with critical acclaim," John factually stated.

"What do you mean another solar system," Bush asked, almost happy that someone else acknowledged life outside of Acirema.

"Well, through my research I have discovered the existence of another galaxy that rotates on a horizontal axis around their sun. The planets in our solar system rotate on a vertical axis in relation to our sun. Every so often, we become a part of this unknown galaxy as their twelfth planet. Of course, my theory has been heavily criticized. They fear of life forms in another solar system."

"So you believe humans exist in another solar system," Bush said, patiently awaiting a response.

"Of course there is life in other galaxies. I have devoted my life to research supporting this fact," Dr. John Rodgers explained.

George smiled a genuine smile for the first time. He could not believe it, someone else besides himself recognized life outside of Acirema. He opened up the floodgates and let out an overflow of information to a curious John Rodgers, explaining events, times and historical facts about his home planet, Earth. He had finally found someone who understood his mind. The two minds exchanged thoughts and theories until the wee hours of the mornings. George told him about Earth and the United States, and Dr. Rodgers educated him on Moja and Acirema. It was a match made in heaven. Finally, he had someone who understood and he could begin to figure out how he got on planet Moja. It all made sense now and George now had a well-needed ally to help him get back to America.

For the first time since he touched down in Acirema, he had a reason to be optimistic. John appeared to be honest and worthy of his trust. Still, he was going to wait a while before he shared his plans of escape. He could not afford another blunder and be discovered. He had too much to lose. It was still a blessing for him to have someone to talk to and not be considered a raving lunatic. At least Dr. Rodgers believed that life could exist outside of planet Moja, and that was a welcome beginning. George would have to spoon feed him information a little bit at a time. He had time because neither one of them had any place to go. He began the appetizer and now John was ready for the full-course meal. George wasn't the only crazy person in Acirema.

"The informant is dead, sir. Danny Sharpe was found boiled in a Jacuzzi at a hotel in Chicago," Prescott announced over the closed circuit phone.

"That's impossible. What the fuck happened? How could they have known that he was an infiltrator," an outraged President Burrows said.

"My men are all over it. We put his death at around 11 p.m. Thursday. We have already questioned Eugene Weems and he has the perfect alibi. He was in Washington preparing for the next One million Man March," Prescott explained.

"Well, I want him arrested anyway. We can't have a CIA agent murdered right under our nose. He's a terrorist!" President Burrows wanted action.

"Well, sir, we can't arrest the new leader of the RNF. It would spark a revolution. It's too soon after the death of Mr. Phillips. Public faith in the government is already at an all-time low." Prescott was pleading by now.

"I don't give a damn. I want this nigger dealt with, and I mean now!" Burrows was fuming with anger.

"Well, sir...sir, let's see how the smear campaign goes and then at least we will have the public behind us. The whole world is watching. We don't want to become another Russia." Prescott was beginning to make sense of the President.

"Well, just do it. I want this nigger boy dealt with, and I mean soon. Terminate him if you have to. Just get rid of him," the President said, impatiently.

"Give me a few more months and I promise that we will have things under control." Prescott was almost confident.

"We don't have a couple of months. I have lobbied for billions of dollars for your agency. I want results." Burrows was almost throwing a tantrum.

"I'm on it. I will see that the situation is handled myself."

"Well, do it, and I mean now. We can't allow these animals to get the upper hand."

A bit of calm eventually prevailed and President Burrows hung up the phone. He sat there in the privacy of the Oval Office, plotting his next move. He hated being one upped by the RNF. He was going to kill Eugene Weems, even if he had to get a knife and do it himself. He actually feared Eugene's power, and in secrecy, longed for a return to the days of Dr. Phillips. There was no telling who would wind up dead next and he didn't want to get caught slipping. His security was at an all-time high, but even Ronald Reagan had been shot. He wanted to squash the RNF before they got more support from the United Nations. Something had to be done. The RNF had just started a war with the most powerful gang in the universe, The American government.

Eugene L. Weems, Timothy R. Richardson

CHAPTER 11

Finally, Doug Winters was going to get his interview with Vice President Condoleeza Kincaid. It was perfect timing, too. His article about the assassination of Dr. Phillips was going to print after a long campaign for his first amendment rights. He had underestimated that geek Cheney Burrows. His power of suppression had stretched to the *Chicago Tribune*. Anybody who said a negative word about him was instantly labeled a terrorist. He had to exhaust all of his resources in Chicago to finally get a sit-down with Vice President Kincaid on her home turf, but he only had 30 minutes with her. Doug could not afford to waste any time. He got right down to business.

"Miss Kincaid, why did you continue to keep your ex-husband's surname?" He had to set the tone.

"I don't believe that you have properly introduced yourself and the organization that you represent." The Vice President was a stickler for journalism etiquette.

"My name is Doug Winters, a freelance reporter with the *Chicago Tribune*."

"I know Carl, and you mean to tell me that he could not even send a staff reporter from my hometown paper?" Condoleeza was almost insulted.

"I wanted the inside story and I'm a Pulitzer Prize winning journalist with over 15 years experience," Doug lied.

"I guess that I'll just have to settle for you, then." Condoleeza had established the tone. She did not want to fall victim to the local tabloids again.

"Well, Ms. Vice President, how does it feel to be the first African American and first woman Vice President of the United States?" Doug played the race card and was going to work his way to the juicy details.

"Well, I don't consider myself the first African American Vice President. I consider myself as just another Vice President." Condoleeza was almost a politician.

"How is your relationship with President Burrows?"

"Well, we have a great working relationship and I support our administration's policies."

"How do you feel about President Burrows' affiliation with known Ku Klux Klan members here in Illinois?"

"Surely, you can't be serious." Condoleeza was shocked.

"Well, I am serious, and on the record. Have you ever heard of the Sons of Liberty?" Doug became more direct. He was almost out of time.

"Who are the Sons of Liberty? What are you talking about?" Condoleeza was even more confused.

"Well, the Sons of Liberty are believed to be a secret organization created by your President. I believe that they were responsible for Dr. David Phillips' untimely death." Doug Winters was now the interviewee.

"That's absurd. What are you talking about? Timothy, get this fool out of my sight!"

In a flash, Doug Winters was thrown out of Condoleeza's home, minus his recorder. He struggled to regain his composure. It wasn't the first time he had been kicked out of someplace. In fact, he had been put out of far better establishments. One thing was certain, either Condoleeza deserved an academy award for her acting or she was clueless to what was going on in the White House. His journalistic instincts believed it was the latter, that Vice President Kincaid had no idea what President Burrows had going on. Doug knew more about what was going on in the White House than she did. He had accomplished his goal and planted the seeds of doubt in the Vice President's head. It was all the ammunition that he needed for his article. He had a few usable quotes that he could include and he still had his notes.

Condoleeza was visibly furious with what had transpired and had just chewed a big chunk out of her press secretary's behind. She could not believe that she had been tricked into giving an interview with such a jerk. Heads were going to roll and somebody was going to pay big time. It took several moments for Timothy to calm her down. She was still steaming. Her world was topsy turvy. She had already been ridiculed in divorce court, and now this. What was Doug Wingers talking about, the Sons of Liberty? What was this secret organization and what role did they play in the death of Dr. Phillips? She had many questions that needed to be answered and the only person that could answer them was sitting in the Oval office in Washington, D.C.

Timothy did his best to calm her down, but Condoleeza was beyond the point of being agitated. He had never seen her so upset in the brief tenure that they had been together. It was as if she were possessed by the devil. He could see horns coming out of her scalp. A metamorphosis had taken place before his eyes. The passive *yes* woman was no more. She was long gone and replaced with a more aggressive, more opinionated woman. Everybody had a breaking point, and obviously the Vice President had reached that level. She demanded answers and she gathered her things so that she and agent Richardson could catch the first thing smoking to the White House. She had a score to settle.

Eugene Weems congratulated Peaches on a job well done. He thanked God for his ability to put plans together. He avoided prison by the skin of his teeth. His alibi of planning the next One million a Month rally had paid healthy dividends. Not even the President was going to take the risk of locking him up in jail. He was too powerful and had too many connections in the United Nations hierarchy. He would get the attention of a living martyr and would make Nelson Mandela's incarceration look like a basket case. The entire world was paying attention to his reparations movement in America. He had a reputation of being a man of peace and talks had already started about him being the recipient of the Nobel Peace Prize.

His dear friend, Dr. Phillips, would have been proud of him. The Black Sphinx was a worldwide organization and membership in the RNF had surpassed 25 million. They came in all shades, colors and economic brackets. The RNF was indeed a force to be reckoned with. His One million a Month rallies were making headlines. Now he had to take things to the next level. His Navy Seal training had taught him that the best attack was a secret attack. He had learned all about the Sons of Liberty and knew about the CIA handshake that ended Dr. Phillips' life. He even knew the secret members who made up the Sons of Liberty. His White House informant was excellent.

He planned his next strike. President Burrows was too risky of a target, especially with the war on terrorism going on. He had too much protection, but Weems could make him feel the sting of the loss of a close ally. Secretary of State Herman Lee was not an untouchable. He was the perfect candidate to be next in line to feel the bite of the Black Sphinx. He picked up his closed circuit radio, "Peaches, I have another victim for you."

Peaches responded, "Yes, your Excellency."

"Herman Eel," the commander voiced.

"As you wish, your highness." Peaches was already on the job.

The leader of the RNF hung up the device and sipped on his herbal tea, already putting together his next alibi. Secretary of State Herman Lee would be lucky if he had an opportunity to see another sunset.

Laura Bush was overwhelmed with the results of the senate race in Georgia. She had won the independent seat in landslide fashion. It was a unanimous victory for the former First Lady. She was glad that she had not changed back to her maiden name because everyone knew of her relationship to George Bush, and finally something positive had come out of being married to him. She now had an opportunity to make a name for herself. Life was looking up for her. She had revitalized her relationship with her parents. The kids were responding very well to their private tutors. She had a promising political career as senator and she was wealthy beyond her wildest dreams. So much had changed in her life. To top it off, she had a new love interest. For the first time in a very long time Senator Bush was having things her way and she was not about to remain content. She was going to have her cake and eat it, too.

London, England

A tall, leggy African American woman was wearing a housecleaning uniform, but she was not a hotel employee. The thought of dressing up like a servant made this politically conscious black woman's skin crawl, but it was very necessary for her to remain anonymous. She pulled out her kit, two normal light bulbs, a syringe, and a quart of gasoline. She filled the syringe with gasoline and carefully injected the fluid into the light bulbs. She then replaced the light bulbs with the two bulbs in the small restroom and departed Room 777 undetected.

That evening, an unknowing Secretary of State Herman Lee checked into a London, England hotel room. He was in town to speak at Oxford University, but really to rally for more support for his anti-reparations cause. He was met at the reception area by a tall leggy Pam Grier type. She flirtatiously smiled and handed him a key. "Room 777," she said, almost impatiently awaiting the surprise that she had waiting for him. The secretary of state snatched the key disrespectfully and went to the elevator. He had no time for games, and he thought of himself as being above black people. The jet lag had gotten the best of him. He wanted to take a leak, shower, shave, and get some well-deserved rest before his day of deceiving the British into rallying behind his cause.

He exited the elevator on the seventh floor with his two bodyguards. He left them at the door where they stood posted like two lampposts. The secretary of state could not be too careful, especially since he had the dual responsibility of controlling the CIA and FBI. He was President Burrows' most trusted ally.

As he reached for the light switch, there was an explosion that shook the room, and Secretary of State

Lee was no more. A slender Pam Grier look-alike was already on the streets of London, navigating her way back to the airport. She got on her closed circuit radio.

"Peaches," a voice said, but didn't need to inquire.

"Mr. Lee is no more," the woman replied.

"Affirmative." Eugene Weems was indeed a man of few words. He hung up the closed circuit radio and continued to sip on his herbal tea halfway across the globe in America. Secretary of State Herman Lee did make it to see another sunset, but not much else.

"Are you fucking kidding me," President Burrows angrily said to Director Prescott, "How could Herman be dead? I just talked to him this morning," he rambled on, still in shock at the news.

"Well, sir, it happened last night in London, an explosion in the bathroom of his hotel room." Prescott had managed to get a few words in.

"I thought he had bodyguards, your best men. What type of protection are you providing us with, Abbott and Costello? You guys are idiots." President Burrows was obviously pained by the loss of his ally. "I want you in my office and I mean immediately!" He slammed down the phone before a response could be made.

The President began to weep like a child who had just lost a bag of priceless toys. He was sick. He had lost his closest ally. How was he going to explain the loss of Herman Lee to the Ku Klux Klan? He was one of their highest ranking officers. He had to get to the bottom of the situation and whoever was responsible was going to pay.

He sat there, frustrated, with the weight of the world on his shoulders. Now he had to explain the situation to the American public. He already had found the perfect solution. He would chalk it up as another battle loss in the war against terrorism. He could lobby for more funds and take an extended vacation at Camp David. He needed some time off and to also search through the ranks of the KKK for a new Secretary of State.

The death of the Secretary of State could not have happened at a more turbulent time. Doug Winters had released another article on the government's conspiracy to kill Dr. Phillips. Mary Ann was threatening to leave her husband unless he came up with more gossip. The RNF had monthly rallies of over one million people on the White House lawn. The House and the Senate both opposed his war on terrorism and called it a hoax. Almost everything was going wrong for the President and it was almost time for re-election.

The President and Prescott met in the confines of the Oval Office. "Mr. President, who do you have in mind to replace Secretary of State Lee?" Prescott waited for the genius to respond.

"Nobody can replace my friend, but I'm going to nominate Phil Rivers."

"Sir, with all due respect, it can't be the same Phil Rivers that I'm thinking of. He is a known white supremacist and has ties to the KKK."

"Yes, it is the same man and I stand by my recommendation. You should be the last person to have anything to say about my nominations. You are a squeeze away from being fired. You can't even protect my people!"

The President had his mind made up already. "Where was Eugene Weems?"

"He was in Chicago at the time of the bombing. His organization did not take responsibility for the Secretary of State's death."

"Of course they wouldn't, you fool. Nobody wants to go to war with the United States of America. We have tax dollars backing us. What does he have?" The President was animated and almost ready to explode. "I want you to silence Doug Winters and then find out who killed Herman. Is that understood?"

"Yes, sir." Nothing else was said and Prescott was shown the door.

President Burrows was alone again. He was silent as he contemplated his next move. He had to do something. His back was against the wall and his entire world was falling apart before his eyes. He got on the phone and called Phil Rivers.

"Hello, is Phil Rivers available," he asked a friendly female voice.

"One moment, please."

The woman's voice disappeared and was replaced by a male voice. "Phil Rivers here, KKK," the voice said. It was almost music to Cheney Burrows' ears.

"Phil, it's the President of the United States." Cheney knew Phil from way back.

"Howdy, President. I heard about brother Lee. That's a damn shame. A white man ain't safe in the universe. How can I help you?"

"That's why I called to offer you the post of my Secretary of State. You are a perfect fit." The President really wanted someone who shared his political views.

After a brief pause, Phil continued the conversation, "Is that post under that nigger? I can't serve under a bitch nigger gal, Cheney. That's inhumane." Phil was adamant about his beliefs.

"There's no way that you will have to answer to her, Phil. Her position is powerless. You will have way more power than she has. Why don't you come to Washington, my treat of course, and we can talk about it over some Jack Daniels."

"Sounds like a plan. I'm on the next flight to Washington. I need to talk to you anyway about your NRA membership." No true redneck could turn down an opportunity to talk politics and sip some free Jack Daniels.

The President hung up the phone, confident that he had himself a new replacement to fill the post of Secretary of State. He was relieved that now there was one less item that he had to deal with. It was going to be hard trying to cope with the loss of his good friend, Herman Lee, but Phil Rivers was racist enough. He was more than adequate replacement.

In a strange way, it turned out to be a blessing in disguise. The President now had all the fuel he needed to add to the fire that would reignite his war on terrorism. Nobody would lobby against him in the Senate or Congress and America wouldn't dare elect a new President in a time of crisis. He was going to blame it on a terrorist group in London and back his accusations religiously, even if it meant going to war with a long time ally. Herman Lee was going to receive a royal send-off worthy of a white knight. The President broke out a fifth of Jack Daniels and poured a tall glass, paying homage to his good friend.

CHAPTER 12

It was a chilly winter day in Chicago. The temperature dwelled somewhere just above 10 degrees. Doug Winters did not want to leave the confines of his heated condo, but he had to get his article printed. He wanted to let the world know about Vice President Condoleeza Kincaid and her ignorance about what was going on in the White House. Despite the weather, the news had to go on. The truth had to be printed.

Condoleeza could not understand what was going on in her complicated head. She had just survived another multi-orgasmic experience with her CIA operative. She had been to bed with several men, but few had learned the art of making love to her like Agent Timothy Richardson. He was more than an expert. He was her soul mate. She never thought in a million years that she would meet her equal sexually. Timothy was like the energizer bunny. He kept going and going, and going. It was the best sex of her life. He made even George Bush look like a clumsy sexual illiterate. She was on the verge of being in love with her protector.

Condoleeza had an increased feeling of security whenever Timothy was near. He had broken down so many barriers to her heart. At first she blamed it on the fact that she was extremely vulnerable after her divorce and almost being relieved of her duties as Vice President. She later realized that it was more than an afternoon affair. She was really attracted to Timothy and they had so much in common. They enjoyed the same movies, liked the same foods, and could converse on topics, like sports, religion and politics. She had found herself thinking of him for hours at a time and she could not keep her hands off of him. She was truly in love for the very first time.

Timothy Richardson was caught between two worlds. He was dedicated to Director Prescott and his allies at the CIA, but he also found himself falling for Condoleeza. It was becoming more and more difficult for him to give his weekly reports on the status of his assignment to his superiors at the CIA. He felt like he was being used by his organization. He felt like he owed Condoleeza his loyalty and didn't want to live the lies that came along with being a CIA operative. At times he felt like a high priced errand boy, a two-dollar whore, a fly in the buttermilk. He knew that Director Prescott secretly hated black people, and Timothy hated the fact that he was being forced to tell the most intimate details, blow by blow, of his relationship with Condoleeza. It was as if Prescott was an insane voyeur, salivating for graphic details of sexual positions and time frames of intercourse.

Timothy Richardson was a leader and was beginning to hate his role as a pawn in the political chess game. He knew a lot about politics and would have made an excellent congressman. Believe it or not, he was beginning to have feelings for the first African American Vice President of the United States. He loved the sense of power that he felt whenever he held her in his arms. The weight of his commitment was beginning to shift in her favor. He felt like he had more than paid his debt to Director Prescott for keeping him out of prison. He no longer feared Prescott's authority and wanted to be his own man again. He no longer liked working for the same system that had oppressed his people for so many years. Timothy Richardson was changing and he no longer hated the reflection that he saw in the mirror. He was beginning to love himself and really like Condoleeza.

As he read the Opinion section of the *Chicago Tribune*, Eugene Weems spotted an article by a contributing reporter by the name of Doug Winters. It talked about the CIA and their long-time rivalry with the RNF. The article blamed the CIA for the death of Dr. David Phillips. It was information that only confirmed what Eugene Weems already knew long before becoming leader of the RNF. He knew because as a former Navy

Seal he was a part of the political bullies known as the American government. He had been on top secret missions and even led his squad on top secret killing assignments. Eugene was not too far removed from being a part of the same system that had oppressed his people. He knew all too well about the ability to silence others that the government possessed and would never make the mistake of underestimating the system.

Eugene Weems was a born leader and had mastered the art of calculated moves. Terminating Secretary of State Lee was a decent beginning, but it was not his definition of revenge for the present administration's assassination of his longtime friend. To even the score, he wanted to fry much bigger fish and he was going to take his time. It was a psychological war that he was fighting. He wanted to break Burrows down to the very last compound. He knew that a coward could not hide forever, and that one day they would have to meet face to face. Until then, Eugene Weems was going to lay low for a while and limit his exposure to the One million a Month rallies. Even the American government was not foolish enough to attack him on the front porch of the White House in front of over one million people.

As a more than capable leader and motivator, membership in the RNF was at an all-time high. Over 30 million people pledged membership worldwide. The RNF was a common household name in America and abroad. Eugene had successfully taken his organization to the next level of leadership, but now he had to lay low for a while, at least until after the death of Herman Lee blew over, and then things could go back to normal.

Eugene Weems had awakened a sleeping giant and he had to be careful before striking again. He knew all too well about the government's power to destroy in the name of terrorism. Now was the time to disappear from the limelight, but that did not mean he was going to remain idle with his time. The truth of the matter was that the leader of the RNF had already planned his next move.

Mary Ann Burrows had enough, she was leaving the President. Things had been going bad for entirely too long. "I can't take this shit anymore, Cheney. You had that good man murdered and now Herman is dead. Who's going to be next, me?" Mary Ann stated.

"Honey, those animals would not be foolish enough to harm my family; on that I give my word," the President pleaded.

"I don't know, Cheney, my life was so much better before coming to Washington. We had so much peace."

"Buttercup, I'm the President of the United States, the most powerful country in the universe. I would never let them harm my family."

"What are you going to do about it? I don't feel safe anymore."

"Well, first of all, I'm going to stop those monthly marches and then I'm going to launch Operation Cyclops." He planted a seed.

"What's Operation Cyclops?" Mary Ann was curious.

"Well, if you leave, you'll never find out," the President strained a smile.

"Okay, but it had better be good."

Mary Ann began to take her bags back into the master bedroom. The President was unsatisfied. He knew his wife like a book and all she wanted was some attention. The death of Secretary of State Lee had everybody walking on pins and needles, including him. He had made the mistake of underestimating his enemies. He blamed the RNF, but he had several enemies that were capable of killing Herman. He had to be careful in his accusations, the RNF was a force to be reckoned with. He did not want to start a civil war on American soil. First thing was first, he had to bury his associate and replace him with Phil Rivers.

He had to get to the bottom of who killed Herman Lee and then deal with them. He was going to miss his ally, but he would eventually get over the loss. Everyone was replaceable, including his First Lady. Everybody had a price and President Burrows had enough money from payoffs to buy whomever he chose. He had learned the political chess game to perfection. His high IQ was already at work concocting a plan to give his wife as Operation Cyclops.

George Bush went into another story about his former life in America. The former doctor listened intently to every detail, probing his imagination for the existence of such a place. It was indeed a world away from Acirema and the reality that stood before these two men daily, but John was optimistic. America fit into his theory about Moja being a visiting twelfth planet in earth's galaxy. It was a theory that he had devoted his life to, and eventually cost him his career as a scientist.

He and George Bush had several conversations and each one was more interesting than the last. They were almost friends and sometimes their conversations in their cell would go on until late into the night. George was finally beginning to open up and he had developed trust in John Rodgers. He was the first person who seemed to bring sense to how he arrived in Acirema. His theory of Moja being a visiting twelfth planet to earth's solar system explained how George had made it to Acirema, maybe he was teleported through this vanity mirror on one of those visits.

"Could you explain your twelfth planet theory again?" George was like a child in Sunday school.

"Well, my twelfth planet theory begins in a moment back in time. The atmosphere of your earth and planet Moja is one and the same. Planet Moja exists as the lone planet in our galaxy. Although we have several moons, we also have our own solar powered star. The only difference is that we rotate on a vertical axis around it. The rotation is such that sometimes we become a part of your galaxy for a period of 24 hours. Scientists from our planet have top secret documentation of visits to your planet you call Earth, but white Aciremans have never laid eyes on it. It remains a pleasure saved for black

151

Aciremans only. Our black astronauts have shared technologies with your once primitive culture, like mysteries of our pyramids, math and fire.

"The documentation of these visits are under lock and key at the Acirema Research Center. They date back hundreds of years to a time known as the ice age. These files have come to be known as the earth files. I would give my right arm for ten minutes to view these files. If what you are saying is true, your people have developed these gifts from Mojan travelers excellently. It is hard to believe that our people control earth. It is more difficult to believe that black people were once enslaved on your planet. Our people have only known that plight here on planet Moja. I find that concept hard to believe and a person could be publicly executed for such absurd thoughts, but I believe you, George. As a scientist, I believe that anything is possible."

"Then help me escape, Dr. Rodgers."

"Nobody has ever escaped from this Acirema prison," the doctor announced.

"Well, I'm confident we can be the first. Have you ever heard of the term, *where there is a will there is a way?*"

"Yes, of course, a black philosopher penned it." .

"Well, I put in a kite for a kitchen job for both of us. I have been doing some observations and there may be a way out through the garbage." George had done his research.

"Well, I'm all for it. It is well worth the risk. I would try just about anything to get out of this vile place."

"All I need is a commitment. Are you with me?" George was almost begging for his support.

"Of course, I'm with you, my alien brother."

The pact was made and now the two men had different priorities. George was going to figure out a way to get out of the hell hole that was his existence. He had a needed ally in Dr. Rodgers. He missed his life on planet Earth. So much time had gone by and he was beginning to worry that his former life was gone forever. He wanted to get back to the peace and tranquility of his Texas estate. He missed his wife and children. He missed bossing his friend, Cheney, around and running his tobacco company. George missed so many things about America, but more than anything he missed having the power of being President of the United States.

Vice President Kincaid was at a crossroads. A lot had happened since her meeting with Doug Winters and the mysterious death of Secretary of State Herman Lee. She wanted to continue her term but did not want to die in the process. She felt secure with Timothy around, but was that enough to keep her alive? Something was obviously going on and she was going to get to the bottom of it. She stormed into the Oval Office, "What's going on? I demand answers," Condoleeza said impatiently.

"What are you talking about, woman," a defensive President Burrows responded.

"Who are the Sons of Liberty? Did you have Dr. Phillips murdered? Am I a token appointment to this administration?" Condoleeza began her verbal attack.

"What...what are you talking about?" Now President Burrows was asking the questions.

"You are a bigot and I don't know why I believed you in the first place! You are a hypocrite and a liar." It was impossible to out-argue a black woman.

"Ms. Kincaid, I need you to calm down if we're going to get to the bottom of this." The President was asking for calm.

Eventually, the Vice President had obtained a certain level of calm. "I was interviewed by Doug Winters and he told me everything."

"I don't believe that you listened to him, of all people. He is a known terrorist and has been a thorn in my side for years."

"Well, I hope that what he said was not true, because if there is even an ounce of truth to his accusations, I resign, effective immediately," Condoleeza said with a serious look on her face. The frustration of being Burrows' punching bag had taken its toll on her. She knew that the public would not accept the Vice President's resignation lightly. There was already a movement to have the President impeached.

"Lies, lies, lies. They're all lies. He is intentionally trying to assassinate my character." Cheney was almost believable.

"I'm giving you one more chance. I understand that your friend has just passed away and things are not going good in your marriage, but if you so much as raise your voice at me, I'm gone. Understand?" Condoleeza was the one making the demands now. She got up out of her seat and left without saying another word.

Cheney Burrows sat at his desk bewildered. He had never been spoken to like that before, not even by Mary Ann. He had to pass the buck, so he called CIA Director Prescott.

"I thought I told you to deal with Doug Winters!" A lot of yelling was going on.

"Well, sir, I'm on it," a stunned Director Prescott responded.

"I don't want you on it, I want it done, and I mean now." The President wanted some immediate results.

"Okay, sir, I will have it taken care of immediately." Prescott heard a loud click from the receiving end of his cell phone.

Later on that evening, while Doug Winters was asleep, three large time released capsules of Drano were inserted into his gas tank. The next morning, Doug Winters went through the routine of inspecting his vehicle. He could not afford to be caught slipping. He had made too many enemies in high places. Bomb-free, Doug began the process of starting his car. He turned the ignition, no response. He turned it a second time and the engine of his Pinto came to life. The gas began to flow and the mixture of liquids was complete. In no time at all there was an explosion and Doug Winters was no more.

Two days later, Condoleeza read the headlines of the *Chicago Tribune* in horror, "Doug Winters dies in car explosion." Condoleeza could not believe the words she read. It was an accident, no fragments were found of any explosives. Condoleeza was relieved that foul play had been ruled out. She sat there in awe. She had just recently had an interview with Mr. Winters. He seemed so alive and full of life it was strange reading about his death. Condoleeza had a newfound appreciation for her life and her relationship with Agent Timothy Richardson. Life was not promised to anyone, not even the Vice President. She closed her eyes and said a prayer for the memory of Doug Winters.

It's early November and Cheney had finally made it to his election for a first full term as President. It had been a very rocky tenure in the White House. He had served during the death of President Bush, Secretary of State Herman Lee, and RNF President Dr. David Phillips. America was a big bundle of confusion under his leadership. The call for reparations had reached a worldwide audience and he was receiving a lot of criticism for not fulfilling George's campaign promise of signing the reparations bill. Eugene Weems had global support for the RNF. Cheney's pleas to Congress to outlaw the One million a Month rallies had fallen on deaf ears. The Supreme Court backed the RNF's right to gather peacefully.

He had stout opposition from Candace Barr, the Democratic contender for the presidency. Election surveys had her winning by a very close margin of victory. If so, Cheney was going to be the first President to lose an election to a woman. The only positives he had going for himself was the war on terrorism and the decision to keep Condoleeza as his Vice President. It was indeed a trying time for President Burrows, and to top things off, his wife had left him.

George was up to his neck in filth. His plan had worked to perfection, although the stench of garbage was all that he could stand. He settled into the mass of refuse, happy to finally be free. The stench was all around him from head to foot. He had never smelled anything like it before, but it was a small price to pay for his freedom. Anything was better than his fate in prison. John had managed to make it along with him. He now had a needed ally in the foreign land of Acirema. They had a lot of work to do plotting his trip back to his planet.

They made it to the city dump and continued their escape. John had a home, but they didn't dare go there. That would be the first place that the authorities would search for them. They had to find a place more remote, somewhere that the police would not look. John had friends that he could depend on. They could plot their moves in secrecy.   George had no idea what the future had in store for him.   He did not know what tomorrow was going to bring.   All that he knew was that he wanted to go back home, and his road home to the comforts of his Texas estate could only be found in one place, the mansion of President Barack Obama.

CHAPTER 13

Condoleeza Kincaid could not believe that she had allowed Burrows to talk her into becoming his running mate. The President was captain of a political ship that was sinking rapidly, but Condoleeza was still loyal to his administration. The fact that Timothy had pleaded with her to stay didn't hurt. Condoleeza was hopelessly in love with Timothy and she would have done anything he asked. He promised to stay on as her personal bodyguard. She was in a better political position also, and was basically telling President Burrows what to do. She had learned how to deal with him for the coward that he was and understood that she meant a lot to his chances of getting re-elected.

Condoleeza loved her newly found sense of power and was not ready to go back to Illinois. After her divorce, and a year from her news anchor position, she preferred the limelight of the political arena. She had a new life in Washington, D.C., her relationship with Timothy was promising. She enjoyed her new role as

Vice President and she could not go back to the monotony of a nine-to-five. Politics was exciting and still new to her. She was still the second most powerful person in the world.

Carl Watson had stumbled over a gold mine when he was cleaning out the desk of his longtime employee, Doug Winters. He had discovered information about President Burrows dating all the way back to his days as an Illinois congressman. Doug had done enough research on President Burrows to write a book. As editor in chief, Carl felt obligated to keep the creative fires burning. Doug was one of his most dedicated employees and over the years they had developed a friendship. He was not going to let his friend's lifelong accomplishment go unnoticed. He was going to keep his memory alive.

He continued to gather information, pictures of Cheney Burrows with high ranking officials of the KKK, recorded conversations between Doug and President Burrows where the President was vocally agitated. It was more than enough evidence to at least make Cheney Burrows a suspect in Doug's death. The more information Carl found, the more infatuated he became with the story. It was rapidly becoming his personal obsession. He was eventually consumed by grief for Doug's memory. Nothing was going to stop him from breathing life into Doug's work. It had become as one with his soul like a young, helpless child left orphaned in this cruel and uncaring world. Carl had the power to

160

make his fallen friend's dream a reality. He was going to make it happen. Doug's passion was now his passion. Doug's enemies were now his foes. He was going to do everything in his power to let the world know about President Cheney Burrows. He was up against a powerful enemy, but he was no powder puff. He had the freedom of press on his side. He was not going to be silenced.

Carl Watson was far removed from his days as a beat reporter. It had been a long and difficult journey on his way to the top of his own newspaper as editor in chief, but his fire was reignited. He had a new purpose. He was still a force to be reckoned with in the publishing world and now he had a listening audience. Getting re-elected was now the least of Burrows' problems.

Back in Washington, D.C., CIA agent Timothy Richardson was beginning to have doubts about his continued commitment to the organization. His little fling with Vice President Condoleeza Kincaid had taken a change for the worse. He was actually beginning to have genuine feelings for her. With each monthly report of the intimate details of their relationship, he was becoming less enthusiastic about his position with the agency. He was a very smart man and he realized quickly that the information that he was providing to Director Prescott was priceless. If it was not for his influence on Condoleeza, she would have never become a running partner with Burrows.

After so many favors and numerous assignments for the CIA, Agent Richardson was fed up. He was tired of brown nosing and believed that he had more than paid his debt to Prescott. He had risked his life on several occasions acting as an informant and he could never show his face again in Columbia. The political bullshit that he had to deal with on a daily basis had taken its toll on him. He was disgusted in the way the nation was being run. The Sons of Liberty used CIA operatives to flood the entire west coast with Mexican heroin. They targeted black communities with their product and they used the money made from their drug trafficking to finance their campaign against reparations. It was a cold game that they were playing with the lives of innocent people. The very same people who were going to benefit the most from the reparations movement funded the strongest movement that opposed the reparations bill.

Timothy had used his remaining cocaine connections as distributors for the CIA project. He was poisoning his own people, but this time it was okay because it was being done for the government. To him, it was still painfully wrong. Rather, it wasn't being done for the government but for Cheney's and Prescott's personal financial gain. He entered through the doors of CIA headquarters and was pointed in the direction of Director Prescott's office.

"Hello, Timothy, have a seat," said a salt and pepper haired man behind the large desk, "How was your flight," Prescott continued. Timothy could sense another favor brewing in the cynical mind of his superior.

"Why did you have me come all the way here from Chicago?" Timothy was curious.

"How are things going with Condoleeza? I hear the two of you are quite an item, like Bobby and Whitney." The director loved throwing shit in Timothy's face.

"Well, I don't care what you heard. It's just another assignment to me. Who is telling you shit about me anyway?" Timothy tried to contain his anger.

"Don't worry my negroid friend, I have eyes everywhere. Remember, I am the director of the CIA."

"Well, if you have eyes everywhere, maybe you can convert some of those eyes to hands and have them push heroin for you on the west coast." Timothy was almost defiant and was wearing his emotions on his sleeve.

"I detect hostility, my little dope-dealing friend. Remember, if it weren't for me, you'd be Nasty Nate's little prison bunkee and under lock and key. I made you! You work for me and don't you forget it!" Director Prescott was an expert at letting Timothy know who was in charge.

"What do you want from me, Mr. Prescott?"

"I want you to start a branch of our distribution network in Chicago. I want you to sell heroin in Chicago."

"What about Ms. Kincaid? I thought my assignment was to protect her."

"Well, your assignment is temporarily over. This assignment is more important."

"Well, what about the Reparations Now Forever? They have headquarters in Chicago and they won't take too kindly to me selling heroin in their communities."

"Fuck the RNF!" Director Prescott was beginning to show his true colors.

"Well, sir, they are a formidable opposition to drug dealers and it's going to be hard to fuck over a million people."

"I will deal with them. You just move my product, understand!" Director Prescott was a bundle of nerves because deep inside he feared the RNF.

"Fine, I'll handle it. Just make sure that somebody of quality protects Vice President Kincaid. Remember what happened to the Secretary of State." It was a well deserved low blow to Prescott's confidence.

As Timothy got out of his chair and made his way toward the exit, he could feel the CIA director's stare piercing his back like knives. He had succeeded in making the director angry, but it paled in comparison to the anger that he was feeling for being transferred. He could not show his true frustration, not just yet. Eventually, Prescott was going to need him again, and right at the point when he needed him the most, Timothy was going to make him beg.

"Sir, Operation Cyclops is in effect. I have just assigned my best agent to the Chicago area."

"Who did you assign?"

"I assigned Agent Richardson."

"Isn't he the same boy you put on Vice President Kincaid?" The President was inquisitive.

"Yes, sir, but I thought that this assignment took priority over the Vice President."

"Don't think. I do all of the thinking for you. I will work things out with her. You just make sure that he takes care of my product, understand."

"Yes, sir, I'm on it." The two conspirators hung up the phone and the President was all alone. He was well aware that the Oval Office, including the telephone calls, was audio recorded 24 hours a day, but he was a genius and it was nothing for him to cause a glitch in the audio recording system.

Operation Cyclops was an excellent concept. The Sons of Liberty were going to flood the country with heroin from Mexico. The CIA was going to provide the manpower needed to distribute the product throughout the black communities and the government would benefit by arresting the street dealers, who would just happen to be black. It would put a black eye in the movement for African American reparations, because the President would use his influence to get funding for the new war on drugs. Nobody would want to give money to black junkies. He then would have additional money to funnel to the CIA to purchase larger quantities of heroin for distribution. In the long run, the President was going to leave the White House wealthy. He would make money from both ends of the war and he was the only one that could see the truth. Thus, Operation Cyclops was born.

President Burrows marveled at his own genius. He had stiff competition in the form of Candace Barr, but not even the American public would dare to vote for a new President during a time of war. He still had a war on terrorism going and now the war on drugs had been activated. He had successfully created enough distractions. The reassignment of Agent Richardson had turned out to be an additional positive. Now the Vice President could focus on her duties and less on her private affairs. Mary Ann had finally came back to the White House. Burrows had successfully rid himself of Doug Winters, and now his image was on a positive upswing. Things were beginning to look good for his re-election.

Condoleeza Kincaid was not happy with the news. Just when things were starting to work out for her and Timothy, he was assigned to another project. The two of them were close, but Timothy would not explain the details of his assignment to her. She just knew that it was classified and he had to go to Mexico for a few weeks. Director Prescott provided her with increased security, but all of the manpower in the world could not replace her love for Agent Timothy Richardson.

After several arguments with President Burrows, she had been promised that Timothy would return to his position after the election. She would have to settle for less for the time being. A lot was going on in her life. Although it was done gradually, Burrows did increase her responsibilities. She was overseeing both the House and Senate during sessions of congress. She traveled less and was more aware of domestic affairs. The elections were coming up and Condoleeza marveled at the fact that she could become the first elected female Vice President. She still appreciated her appointment, but being elected to office was a completely different story.

After further thought, she could afford to let the flame of her love affair with Timothy die down a bit, but not too much. She was just beginning to finally have someone that she could trust. She felt comfortable being herself around Timothy. Maybe Cheney was right to reassign Timothy for a little while; now she could focus on her duties. She was so confused. So much was at stake in the upcoming election and she didn't need any distractions. On the other hand, she didn't have anyone that she could trust and she felt all alone. She could not let loneliness get the best of her because her love affair with Timothy was still a secret. The last thing in the world she wanted was to let the President know what was going on between them.

Condoleeza kicked back and let down her hair a bit in preparation of the long night ahead of her. She was in the all too familiar position of being an outcast. Things were so much better when she had Timothy there as a protector and to share her thoughts with. She missed him already, but being the Vice President was a very lonely job. It was a job that she was getting well-acquainted with and that she was beginning to like. Being without her sex partner caused an itch deep within her womb that needed to be scratched. She was alone and at the peak of horniness, and wished that Timothy was there to scratch that itch. She took a long, hot shower in anticipation of the long days that were ahead of her without her comfort, without her joy. Condoleeza longed for the warmth of his strong, hard body. As she lay alone in bed, a wetness overcame her pulsating vagina. She longed for the comforts of her man, so she optioned for the next best thing. She reached in her drawer and pulled out her vibrator.

Eugene Weems had pulled off the assassination of the Secretary of State, but still the black warrior was not satisfied. His accomplishment was mere crumbs in the political game and he wanted the whole pie. He wanted another victim higher on the political food chain. He firmly believed in the concept of an eye for an eye. After all, the CIA had taken the life of his closest friend and most trusted ally. Something more had to be done. He had to strike them where it hurt the most. It was also very apparent to him that he had to wait until after the election to implement the next phase of his plan.

The upcoming election did not look good for President Burrows anyway. Many political observers predicted stiff competition from Candace Barr. He wanted to be patient and wait for the outcome before making his next move. For now, he had to keep a low profile and remain out of the public's eye. He was going to kick back and watch the race for the White House from afar, but he was going to keep a very close eye on Cheney Burrows. He knew that Cheney was desperate to remain in office as President. He also knew that desperate people did desperate things.

Laura Bush was a Georgian senator. She had never imagined in all of her years that she would have thrown her designer hat into the world of politics. She observed her new Atlanta mansion with the pride of a first-time mother. It was a new and beautiful beginning for Mrs. Bush. Power was finally hers for the taking and she relished the feeling. For the first time in her life, she felt respected and people liked her for who she was. Jenna and Barbara even expressed their happiness in the change they saw in their new mother. The kids were excelling with their tutor and loved their new environment. Laura had everything she dreamed of. After so many years of putting up a front in vain attempts to satisfy others by living a lifestyle far over her head, it felt good to finally be independent and on her own. Many people envied the life she led as the wife of a billionaire. If only they knew the truth. She would have easily traded a week of her present life for an eternity of her former life. Life with George was not as wonderful as the public thought.

The only good thing about her past was that it was now far behind her. She now had a beautiful present and even a more wonderful future. Life was looking bright for her and she finally liked the woman she saw in the mirror. Everybody noticed the change in her, and the change was for the better. She was a United States senator, representing her home state of Georgia. She still could not believe it when she thought about how far she had come. Her position of power would enable her to make decisions that would affect the lives of millions of people. She had made up her mind that she was going to be a far better politician than George ever was. She was going to keep all of her campaign promises, education, housing for the homeless, and yes, supporting the reparations bill. At last, she was going to do things that she never believed she would be capable of doing if George were alive. She was going to help out the less fortunate.

Laura followed the RNF and was by now a stern supporter of the movement. She had developed her own political personality and felt comfortable with who she had become. The reparations movement was a worthy cause that she felt would benefit the country. She figured that Native Americans had sovereign land and the Japanese had received reparations for the horrors suffered in World War II, so African Americans more than deserved their share of the American pie for 400 years of slavery. She had witnessed the oppression African Americans had suffered being passed down from generation to generation, growing up in the south. Laura wanted to change that trend by doing what she could to support the cause. After living so many years under the harsh rule of George Bush, she was very familiar with the feeling of being an oppressed woman. She identified with not being able to express her views and being treated like a second class citizen, but now she was finally free.

Eugene L. Weems, Timothy R. Richardson

CHAPTER 14

The Presidential debate had turned out to be a nightmare for President Cheney Burrows. It was impossible for him to try to win an argument with a woman, and Candace Barr was no ordinary woman. She was an educated and independent woman that had an opinion about almost everything. Cheney only had two positive things going for him. One, he had taken over for a fallen President. Two, he had managed to keep Condoleeza Kincaid as his Vice President. Other than that, the Presidential debate was borderline slander on the President's persona. He couldn't answer any questions about his war on terrorism and his domestic performance was brutally criticized. He was so disappointed in his performance that he had fired all of his political advisors.

Cheney Burrows sat alone in the privacy of the Oval Office and couldn't help but wonder if his days in the White House were numbered. His entire political world was crumbling before his eyes and he didn't see an end in sight to the chaos. He had to do something to stop the landslide of frustrations coming his way. He got on the phone and contacted CIA Director Prescott.

"What is the status of Operation Cyclops?"

"We have our connection in place and expansion is going well."

"How are the figures going? What's the bottom line?"

"We have surpassed the $100 million dollar mark in profits. The natives are eating product up like candy. Every nigger in Chicago is going to have cavities." The CIA director was more than proud of his accomplishments.

"Good, good. Well, increase production. I want distribution doubled." President Burrows knew he was living on borrowed time.

"Yes, sir, as you wish. Your wish is my command." The CIA director sensed the urgency in Cheney's voice.

"Well, get on it," the President said, and hung up the phone.

Benson, the hired help, entered the Oval Office with a smile, "Sir, may I get you anything?" It was late night and the mood was gloomy.

"Yeah, son, Jack Daniels, no ice. Bring the bottle."

Benson was old enough to be his father, but he left the room without comment. Burrows sat alone, contemplating his next move. He was a slight underdog in the election and had less than two weeks to change his position. His marriage was on the rocks and he had become bored with Mary Ann's obsession with gossip. The RNF was a political thorn in his ass, but he could not terminate Eugene Weems without bringing negative attention to himself. Everybody knew about the One million a Month marches and how he had tried everything in his executive power to end them. To top things off, Candace Barr had become an opponent to be reckoned with.

Benson returned with a silver platter on which sat a fine bottle of Jack Daniels whiskey. He set it on the President's Oval Office desk, "Anything else, sir?"

"Leave me!" The White House butler was shooed away like an un-tipped waitress at a strip club.

The President retrieved the bottle of whiskey from the silver platter and long-throated it straight from the bottle. He was pleasantly intoxicated in no time at all. He sat alone in a drunken wave of depression and thought about what his life had become. He had lost all hope of accomplishing true happiness. His best friend had mysteriously disappeared without a trace. His ally of many years had been murdered and he had no idea who had committed the act. His wife's mouth ran like a leaky faucet, and everyone around him seemed incompetent. He thought about ending it all and regretted the day that he took over as President.

A lot was at stake in a couple of weeks. His reputation was on the line, a Yale Law School graduate could not dare lose an election to a female. The more Cheney drank, the more he wanted to escape his miserable existence. He wondered how his good friend George would have handled the situation and took another swig of whiskey. He had two short weeks to get his act together or for the first time in his Rhodes Scholar life he was going to be in the unemployment line.

George marveled at the pleasure of a private shower. It was a luxury that he would never take for granted again. They had finally made it to the safety of John's Acirema home. John had arranged for them to stay with his family for a few hours, but they had to move on before they were discovered by the authorities. George took in the humble surroundings. The small township where white Aciremans lived was a far cry from the lavish country clubs that he owned membership to back in America. It was indeed a step down for George, but anything was better than life in an Acirema prison. He savored his freedom.

George noticed how common John's life was as a scientist. He had an average looking wife and a few kids, but nothing about his life was out of the ordinary. In America, a white scientist would be wealthy. George had hired and fired several during his tenure at Bush Industries. It was very apparent that whites had a separate lifestyle in Acirema. He noticed neighborhood graffiti, pollution, and the omnipresence of black police. There were hourly helicopter patrols and he felt unsafe. The interesting thing was that he had not seen one black face in the white township.

He was already calculating his next move. He had been in Acirema long enough and wanted his living nightmare to end. He was going to do whatever it took to get back home to the comforts of his billionaire lifestyle. With him being gone for so long, he wondered how his family was doing without him. He wondered if he was being remembered, or had he been forgotten like a used postage stamp.

Time was running out for their stay at John's house. They had to get out and find another place to hide, "John, do you have any other friends that you can depend on?" George was desperate to keep moving.

"Yes, I have a colleague named Jeff Day who lives on the other side of town. He may help us. I'll give him a call." John picked up the phone and dialed a secret number. He talked for a few minutes, almost arguing, but eventually hung up with a smile. "He said we could hide out there for a few days, but then we would have to move on." John was satisfied with himself.

"Thank goodness. It shouldn't take that long to plot our trip back to America." George already had a plan in mind.

"Here, put these on." John threw George a fresh change of clothing. They were about the same height and had a similar physical build.

"Thanks." George went into the bathroom for yet another shower, and to change.

John said his goodbyes to his wife and kids, got some food and money, and they were off. It was not a second too soon. As they left the confines of his home, a news bulletin was flashed on the television with a picture of him and George. They were officially fugitives and were said to be armed and dangerous. They no longer had the luxury of being anonymous and there was even a reward for their capture. They left in Jennifer's car and headed for their next location.

George was on the run and felt like a hunted deer. For the first time in his life, he could not buy his way out of a situation. He was totally dependent on John for his existence and it was not a good feeling. George was still hesitant about trusting people in Acirema, but he knew that he could not do it alone. He had to get someplace where he had a few minutes to gather his thoughts and then he could perfect his plan of escape. The only thing on his mind was getting back to the United States and the confines of the White House. He was already thinking of ways to reward John, who had put his life on the line to help him get home.

He glanced out of the car's window at the impoverished homes and abandoned streets. It was a totally different world from the beautiful land that surrounded the mansions where President Barack Obama lived. After a few days in hiding, George was going to figure out how to get to that land. He knew that it was his only way home and away from the hell hole that was Acirema. George only had one thing in mind, how was he going to get into that mansion and find his way back to that vanity mirror undetected?

CHAPTER 15

The election was too close to call and it had come down to the State of Texas. The electoral votes were virtually a tie going into the Lone Star State. The entire situation made Cheney as nervous as a chicken in the hood the day before payday. He was fortunate that he had an ally in the governor's mansion in Austin, Texas. Early indicators had Candace Barr ahead by a large margin while the votes were being tallied. It was no secret that Texas was going to be the deciding state, and whoever won Texas was going to win the election.

Cheney made a call to his old Yale friend, "Hey, Tex McClure, how ya doin'? It's Cheney Burrows."

"Hey, Cheney, how are things in the White House? Long time no hear from you." Tex really didn't like Cheney.

"I'm shitin' bricks, Tex. Didn't know this dame had it in her. Looks like the gateway to the White House is going to run through Texas." Cheney had a hint of kiss ass in his voice.

"Is that so."

"Things aren't looking too good for me. I need a favor."

"How big of a favor?"

"I need to win this election. I'll make it worth your while, but you have to make it happen for me, brother." It was a certain way that he used the word *brother*.

"I need 20 million to make it happen for you."

"Not a problem." The presidency was worth more than that. Four more years of dealing heroin was going to make Cheney half a billion dollars. The two conspirators hung up the phone.

Cheney sat back in the Oval Office and watched the news coverage of proceedings in the utmost confidence, now that he had successfully fixed the election. The announcement came in no time, the ballots were now being counted in top secret. The entire nation was looking at Texas. All other states had already announced their winners. Candace Barr led the popular vote by one million votes and was ahead in electoral votes by ten. She only needed a few more votes to get the necessary votes to become the first female President of the United States.

He watched CNN as news swept across the country, "Presidential race comes down to Texas." The news began to dominate every channel. There had never been an election so close. The fact that the deciding electoral votes were in Texas placed all eyes on the Lone Star State. Burrows was relieved that he had connections in high places, and that he had paid his annual dues to the KKK. Governor Tex McClure had pulled the plug on the election and was performing a mass recount of all the ballots. It would just so happen that all of the ballots with Candace Barr as President were found to be invalid. So as a result, Cheney Burrows won the popular vote in Texas by a landslide, thus won the final electoral votes to become President.

The entire nation was in an uproar. Candace Barr demanded a recount and everybody pointed the finger at Tex McClure for fixing the election. However, nobody could prove anything to the American public. Justice had been done as far as the President was concerned. After all, President Burrows was already in the White House, so who were the critics going to complain to? He had pulled off the biggest political upset in history and nobody could challenge his victory. He had stolen the presidency away from Candace Barr in broad daylight.

It was official, Cheney was elected to the presidency. It was one less problem he had to deal with. Four more years of vacation at the expense of the American taxpayers. Four more years of expanding his war on terrorism as a camouflage to cover up the heroin distribution network of the Sons of Liberty. His marriage problems were over. Mary Ann was just in a panic because she feared that he was going to lose the election. Now that he was elected President, she was going to be back on his jock for gossip. Cheney swallowed down the last of his Jack Daniels and called Benson for another round. He had pulled off the upset of the century. Now it was time to celebrate.

Condoleeza Kincaid jumped into the arms of Timothy Richardson. It had been done, her dreams had been realized. She had been elected Vice President of the United States. Tears of joy streamed down her cheeks as she showered her man with passionate kisses. She was still in disbelief and had no idea how Cheney had pulled it off, but she was elated nonetheless. Now she was official. The stigma was removed from her name in the history books. Nobody could say that she was a political whore placed in office as a token appointment. She had won the Vice-Presidency outright. Now it was time to celebrate with her man.

The days spent away from Timothy were some of the most difficult days of her life. She had her mind made up. From now on she was going to make the decisions. She was not going to play political flunky to Cheney Burrows and CIA Director Prescott. Decisions made by her were going to be accepted whether the powers that be liked them or not. She had made up her mind.

"Timothy, will you marry me and make me the happiest woman in the world?" The Vice President caught her bodyguard by surprise.

"You're kidding me, right?" Timothy was shocked beyond belief.

"Of course I'm not kidding, silly, let's get married." Condoleeza was serious.

"I feel for you, but I cannot marry you right now."

"What do you mean you can't marry me?" Her anger began to boil, and before long her tears of joy were replaced with tears of sadness.

"Well, the time is not right. I'm still working on my assignment in Chicago and Los Angeles."

"Fuck your assignment. I can't believe that you would put your CIA shit before my feelings."

"Condoleeza, Condoleeza, what do you want me to do? I have obligations to tend to," Timothy was explaining himself.

"What else do I expect you to do? I expect you to tend to the obligations you have with me."

"Well, I can't marry you, Condoleeza. I'm sorry." Timothy had his mind made up. In his role as a CIA informant, he had rules to follow.

"If that's how you feel, get the fuck out of my house and stay the fuck away from me, Timothy!"

"Condoleeza, I'm sorry."

"Get out, I mean it! Leave right now!"

Timothy gathered his things and left. He had never seen Condoleeza so upset. He hoped that he had made the right decision. Director Prescott was going to have his head on a platter. He had invested a lot of time into breaking down the barriers and gaining her trust. Another agent was not going to be able to make the same progress. It was going to take time. He wished that Condoleeza did not put him in the position to make such a critical decision.

He got out his cell phone, "Good evening, Mr. Director." Prescott was awakened from his sleep.

"This had better be good, son." The director was not one to play games.

"I've been fired by Condoleeza Kincaid, sir."

"She what! She can't fire you. I do all the hiring and firing around here!" Now the CIA director was wide awake.

"What is my next course of action, sir?"

"Well, boy, you fucked up big time. What happened that made her flip?"

"She asked me to marry her, sir."

"That girl done lost her mind! You go to Chicago and move my product. Lay low for a few months and I will handle this bitch."

"Yes, sir."

"And Richardson?"

"Yes, sir."

"As long as your are black don't ever call me at home with your bullshit!" The phone went dead.

Condoleeza was in the all too familiar position of being alone again. She began to wonder if she had been too hard on Timothy or maybe she was moving too fast. It had never happened to her before. She was hopelessly sprung on someone that apparently did not feel the same way. How could he have played with her emotions like that? She thought he was different, but he turned out to be like all the rest of the men in her past. She was hurt beyond belief and now a big void filled the space where her heart once beat. So much had happened and her head was spinning. She went from a feeling of victory to a feeling of despair. Now she wished that she had never met Agent Timothy Richardson.

Condoleeza went through a rollercoaster ride of emotions and pondered her next move. Like it or not, she was going to have to go on without Timothy and live with her decision. After all, she was still Vice President of the United States. Life had to go on. She was already plotting her revenge on Timothy for breaking her heart so painfully. She was a woman scorned and no anger in the world could compare to the fury of a black woman scorned.

Eugene Weems knew that something was fishy and it stank all the way to the White House. He had underestimated the desperation of the President and it had been a very long time since the leader of the RNF was wrong. He wanted Candace Barr to win the election, and that meant a more liberal and understanding person in the White House. Now he had to deal with the horror of four more years of Cheney Burrows and he would have to fight tooth and nail to have the reparations bill passed. Mr. Weems had watched the entire scenario unfold from the confines of his Bay Area mansion. This Presidential election was like getting to the race track to witness a horse race, and the favored horse was tripped up at the finish line. The RNF commander in chief had his work cut out for him, but Eugene Weems loved a challenge. Nothing ever came easy for him and it was not about to start now. Challenges kept this warrior on his toes and Cheney was a major challenge. It was too bad that the President was on the other side. Eugene thought that maybe in another life they could have been friends, but only if his skin color was a lighter pigmentation.

Eugene Weems began to focus his thoughts on alternative means of getting his reparations bill passed, but even for him it was going to be impossible to do it without the President's support. Any way he looked at it, the President was not going to sign the reparations bill voluntarily. The only way he was going to cooperate was through force. He had to find a way to force him to sign his legislation. The One million a Month rallies were working and bringing attention to the call for reparations, but he needed to work another angle. Mr. Weems wanted an alternative that was going to bring faster results.

Cheney did not want the memory of his fallen friend to disappear without a struggle. Now he was again a powerful man and everybody knew about his hatred of the RNF. It was only a matter of time before he sic'd both the CIA and FBI on the RNF. He was not going to rest until the RNF was officially dismantled, especially after the death of his partner in crime, Secretary of State Herman Lee.

Eugene Weems knew that the President was already planning his course of action. A war had been started and he knew that he had a powerful foe in President Burrows, but Eugene was no cupcake. He had been battle ground proven. His business was taking names and kicking asses, and up to this point in his life, business had been very good.

Laura was living a bittersweet life. Her life was bitter because she was outraged at a system that allowed a President to swindle his way into office. Life was sweet because the same system had allowed her to become a Georgia senator with no political experience. How did Cheney get elected President of the United States? It was a question that was not only on her mind but it was also on the minds of millions of American voters. The only two people who knew for sure were Cheney and Tex McClure in Texas, and she was sure that they were not telling any secrets anytime soon.

Despite the disheartening news, Laura's life was on an upswing. She had successfully gotten her Atlanta mansion up to her still lofty expectations. The kids were now enrolled in school and now she had more time to focus on her political career. She supported the RNF and Eugene Weems, a thing she could have never done if her racist husband was still alive, but that was the life of the old fearful Laura Bush. The new independent Laura was unafraid to stand by her beliefs.

The only thing negative about her new life was the fact that she did not have male companionship. It was not because of looks either. She was beautiful and had many men who admired her from afar, but she could not trust anyone. She had no idea who was with her for her personality and who was with her for her fortune. It was the main reason that she had grown attracted to Tony Gibson. She was around him often and she had grown very fond of him. Tony was tall, black, strong and very handsome. He was very smart, too. He and Laura would get involved in deep conversations about a variety of issues and she enjoyed his company. She had never slept with a black man before, so she did not know how to take their relationship to the next level. Often, she would feel as awkward as a little girl in high school with a crush on a star athlete. Tony was a challenge and she loved challenges.

They were engaged in one of their many moments alone, she decided to make her move. "Tony, how would you feel if I told you about someone who liked you," Laura nervously exposed.

"Well, it depends on who that someone was." Tony didn't have a clue.

"Well, what if that someone was a person who you worked for?" Laura was tired of playing games.

"What do you mean someone I worked for? I only work for you." Tony was beginning to get the clue.

"Tony, I find you very attractive and intelligent. Would you like to sleep with me?" She got straight to the point.

"I...I don't know what to say," replied a stunned Tony. He was backed into a corner.

"You don't have to say anything, just lay back and I will do all the work."

Laura untied the tie on his no-question designer suit. She pressed her lips against his and she felt kissed for the first time. It had been so long since she had been penetrated and felt the comforts of a man. Tony was a more than willing participant as he touched parts of her body that had never been touched by black hands before. The two of them made love well into the night and her body erupted into climax after earth shattering climax. It felt so good for her to finally release her sexual tension.

The next morning, the two sexually satisfied lovers lay next to each other in Laura's Atlanta mansion. She was mad at herself for waiting so long to indulge in the pleasures of a black man. Tony had turned out to be a wonderful treat in waiting. She had never experienced sex like that before, not even in her wildest dreams. Now it was an addiction that was as dominant as any urge she had ever experienced in life. Laura had to have her chocolate and now she knew where the popular cliché came from, *once you go black you never go back*, and Laura went black over and over again.

Eugene L. Weems, Timothy R. Richardson

CHAPTER 16

Agent Timothy Richardson was caught between a rock and a hard place. On the one hand, he had what was turning into a lifelong commitment to the CIA and Director Prescott. On the other hand, he had his relationship with Condoleeza Kincaid, the Vice President of the United States. In one relationship he was being used by the CIA to peddle drugs into the black community. In the other relationship he was being used by the CIA to get information from an attractive but naïve African American woman. He wasn't a dummy, so it didn't take him long to realize that he was being used by the CIA. He had to do something to stop this vicious cycle of debt and to mend things up with Condoleeza. He was at the point in his life where he felt that he no longer owed Director Prescott and wanted to sever ties with his organization. He felt that he had paid his debt because he had risked his life and destroyed several lives for the CIA.

He had made the mistake of getting his heart involved in an assignment. He was beginning to fall in love with Condoleeza. As he tried his best to focus on the task at hand of delivering 20 kilos of heroin to his Los Angeles connection, he had to clear his mind from the negative thoughts of the double life he was living, because the streets of South Central Los Angeles were tough, especially for a black man. Many rumors had began to circulate about his allegiance to the CIA and he could not afford for his cover to be blown. If it were, his life expectancy was about 20 seconds. The street gangs in LA that he dealt with would not hesitate to kill a CIA agent. Mr. Richardson did not want to become a notch in some street thug's belt.

He tried to remove the thoughts of Condoleeza, but they continued to haunt his mind and spirit. How could he have taken her for granted? He should have seen that she was looking at it as more than a casual sexual relationship. He should have seen it coming and had a reaction planned. Now he had fucked things up big time and Prescott was involved in the situation. He began to have second thoughts about involving the CIA director. Prescott did not care about him or Condoleeza Kincaid. All he cared about was making money off the black community and kissing the ass of President Burrows.

He should have allowed things to cool off and then approach Condoleeza with a solution. He should have never taken her feelings for granted and backed himself into a corner. Now things were fucked up big time. Many scenarios of how to clean things up went through his mind. He knew that he was going to be put back on the assignment. Condoleeza didn't trust anybody else with her safety.

George Bush had been on the run for a few weeks and was tired, frustrated and ready to get home to America. His life was a fragment of what it used to be as time seemed to stand still. As a wanted man, he could not afford to stay in any one location for extended periods of time. Fortunately, he was blessed with a friend who believed in America by now almost as much as him. The scientist in John wanted to explore this new and exciting world. The task of helping George escape Acirema was a small price to pay for admission to a wonderful and new world.

The two fugitives had found refuge in a small town named Atokad at John's sister Penelope's house. Penelope was a housekeeper for one of the black dignitaries. She had a good standing in the black community and the police would never suspect her of harboring fugitives. George welcomed the opportunity to settle down for a few moments on friendly soil. The prison had released a nationwide photo of George and John as wanted men. As a result, they had to lay low for a while and plan their next course of action.

Penelope was young, but very attractive. George took an instant liking to her. The fact that he had not seen a decent looking white woman in two years didn't hurt either. He had almost forgotten how attractive the opposite sex could be.

"So you are from a place called the United States?" Penelope was rather inquisitive. She looked as though she were in her early twenties.

"Yes, that is my home and I can't wait to get back." George was nervous expressing himself to such an attractive woman.

"John has told me all about this place that you speak of. It's hard to believe, a place where black people were once slaves. It sounds insane to me."

"Well, it's true. White people control the world where I come from. They control the politics, money, and everything else. I was the President of my country and a very wealthy man."

"It still sounds crazy. My brother got locked in an insane asylum for such absurd talk. It seems that he has found someone just as loony as him. I wish you two the best of luck."

"I am not crazy! The world I describe is real!" George was offended and the frustration showed in his eyes.

"I..I'm sorry. I did not mean to offend you, but I will not tolerate you yelling at me in my own house. I'm just trying to help you."

John had come into the room with a confused look on his face. "Is there a problem," John said, looking at George.

"No, my brother, we were just having a conversation about this America. Isn't that right, George?"

"Yes, sure, and I just got a little excited about getting home. Sorry for the disturbance," George said, looking directly in the eyes of Penelope. John still sensed that something was wrong and he still did not fully trust George, so he asked Penelope to fix them a meal.

He and George then retreated to the den and began a different conversation.

"George, I would like for you to remain in my company, but I will not tolerate any disrespect to my sister. Is that clear?"

"Yes, John, I understand, but she has a twisted belief in my society."

"I realize that, but here in Acirema, men like us have views that are in the minority. You must be patient with the others. Remember that we are the misfits. We are the escaped prison inmates. We are the ones who are on the run."

"Okay, John, I'm sorry. It won't happen again."

George had already apologized more in the past hour than he had in his entire life in America. The two men now had a better understanding. George had to realize that his money wasn't any good in Acirema and that John was helping him out of sheer speculation. Nothing was promised to either of them. George wasn't guaranteed to get home and John was still not totally certain of his theory about the twelfth planet. If George was going to make it home from Acirema, he was going to have to keep his comments to himself, a skill that he was beginning to utilize more and more.

195

The year was 2005 and Cheney Burrows was the newly elected President of the United States. It was an immaculate inauguration ceremony with all of the trimmings; country and western music, white celebrity guests, and the excitement of a king's coronation. All of Cheney's political allies were present and Tex McClure stood right by his side. Condoleeza Kincaid was like a fly in buttermilk. The only other blacks present were there in a service capacity, but Cheney didn't care. It was his vision of America, his vision of the future.

Later that day, Cheney sat alone in the White House, satisfied with his conquest of the American political system. He had successfully purchased the presidency of the United States for twenty million dollars. He was still in shock at what money could buy. The thought had never occurred to him that he was elected because of his vision. Everybody knew that he had won his post because of white America and his war on terrorism. He had used fear to get the white vote and there had been enough deaths during his first tenure as President to spark enough interest in homeland security. He had successfully fooled the American public again.

He relished in his role as the leader of the Sons of Liberty. They had expanded their heroin distribution network throughout Chicago and Los Angeles. By the time his second term as President came to an end, he would have made over a billion dollars for his organization, well needed funds to fight the RNF and to set him up lavishly for the rest of his life. After his presidency, he had goals of traveling the world and buying him a few wives from third world countries to cater to his every whim. He was successfully on top of the world.

He had only one major problem that was still nagging him now that the election was over. He had continued to make ludicrous promises to back the reparations bill. It was the only way for him to get the white liberal vote. Many of his followers were going to want him to follow through on his campaign promise. He was far from willing to do anything to help the RNF. They were his lifelong enemy and he was certain that Eugene Weems and his flunkies had something to do with the death of his former Secretary of State. He vowed his opposition to the RNF and anything that they stood for. He was going to find a way to bring them down if it was the last thing that he did.

Now was the time to take America to the next level of his leadership. He had to find another way to get to Eugene Weems and topple the RNF. He sat in the confines of the Oval Office and contemplated his next move. He decided to call a meeting of the Sons of Liberty, where he would unveil the plot to destroy the RNF. He was not about to allow them to have monthly meetings on the White House lawn and take away from the glory of his presidency. The RNF was a thorn in his ass that he wanted surgically removed. It was the only black eye to his administration and something had to be done.

Condoleeza had lived through the horror of the President's inauguration and even for her it was as boring as Wednesday night bingo. However, it still did not overpower the joy in her heart of being elected to the Vice-Presidency. She was very comfortable in the fact that she was one of the main reasons that Cheney was elected. Had it not been for her skin color and the fact that she was female, Cheney would not have received the republican female vote, and he desperately needed every vote that he could get. Now that the election was behind her, she could begin to focus on her responsibilities to bring change to America. She would step up her presence and influence in Congress. It was unfortunate that despite promises of the contrary that she would work closely with the CIA and the FBI.

For some reason, she was allowed access to those organizations and was beginning to think CIA Director Prescott was hiding something. Even she knew that the CIA was a top secret organization and there was a very elite fraternity that she did not belong to, but as Vice President she was going to break the trends. She was on a roll and believed that she could shock the world. Her personal life was a mere shadow of her political life in the limelight.

Everybody wanted a piece of the first African American female Vice President. She was a hot item on all the media circuits and everyone desired her presence on their interview couch. Oprah Winfrey, David

Letterman, Tavis Smiley, Jay leno, Tyra Banks, and even Dr. Phil requested the presence of the lovely Condoleeza Kincaid. She had received book offers, movie scripts, and even an offer to pose nude in *Playboy Magazine*. She was the talk of the town.

One day, while going through her fan mail, she came upon a letter. She opened it, *"You black nigger bitch, go back to Africa or we are going to kill you for messing up our white world."* Condoleeza was in shock. Someone had made a threat on her life. It was something that had to be dealt with. She didn't know what to do. Cheney had too much on his mind in dealing with the RNF and hiding his affairs. She did not want to bring it to his attention. He did not care about her safety. The next thing she thought was getting in contact with Timothy Richardson. It had been some time since she had last talked to him and she missed him dearly, especially now.

She called him on his cell phone, "Timothy," she said, waiting for a response.

"Yes, who is it?" He already knew who it was. Only a few people had his private number.

"This...it's me, Condoleeza."

"How can I help you? Congratulations on your election. I saw you on TV." He almost seemed genuine.

"Thanks, Timothy. That was not my reason for calling. I have an emergency." She got straight to the point.

"What's your reason for calling then," Timothy inquired.

"Today, I received a death threat and I want you back." There, Condoleeza had made the first move.

"That's a decision I have to talk over with my director."

"Timothy, please don't be that way. I know that I overreacted. I made a mistake. I apologize."

"Well, let me think about it," and the phone went dead.

Condoleeza stood there, staring at the phone in disbelief. She quickly re-dialed the number and got voicemail. It was obvious that Timothy was screening his calls. Now she was upset again. She could not believe that he would have the nerve to hang up on the Vice President of the United States. She was the one that was used to playing hard to get and she did not like being on the receiving end of punishment. It dawned on her that maybe she had placed too many emotions in the hands of an idiot, but she knew Timothy too well. He was expressing his emotions the only way that he knew how, being cool and collected. Nothing seemed to upset Agent Timothy Richardson. She hated to admit it, but that was one of the main reasons, besides his antics in bed, that she adored him.

She had to admit that the death threat was as good an excuse as any to contact her lover. Time away from him was very lonely indeed. It had been entirely too long since she had experienced a heartfelt orgasm and she knew that Timothy was the remedy. She was long over the rejection that she had felt after being denied his hand in marriage. She viewed her attitude as being immature and had realized the error of her ways. Condoleeza had messed up a very good thing. Now she longed for the protection that she got from Timothy. She wanted to feel his strong embrace and for him to tell her that everything was going to be all right. Even as Vice President, she still did not feel the comfort that Timothy gave her. After further thought, her mind was made up and she was not going to rest until she got her man.

Eugene Weems was not feeling too well. He had just received a court order from the federal government outlawing his One million a Month rallies. He knew that President Burrows was behind the opposition to his organization, but his hands were politically tied. Mr. Weems was not going to take his medicine sitting down. He had already devised a plan to take his struggle to a large audience. He was going to take America to an international court. His case for reparations was going to be heard by the United Nations.

The RNF infiltrator at the White House had already told him about the Sons of Liberty's plot to distribute heroin in black communities in Chicago and Los Angeles. Eugene was curious about the rapid rise in heroin addicts in his communities and now he knew who was behind it. The heroin situation had worked its way to the forefront as a major concern of the RNF. Blacks were becoming addicted to the drug at record numbers. Even Mr. Weems was surprised to find out that President Burrows and his crew were behind it, but he could not expose the Sons of Liberty until he had more evidence. Besides the disheartening news, Reparations Now Forever was still a force to be reckoned with.

With the travesty of the Presidential election behind him, Eugene could come back to the forefront of the struggle. His second in charge, Kendu Marley, had been doing an excellent job in his absence, but it was time for him to come forth. It was time for Eugene to strike, and strike hard with a vicious blow. The RNF had been ignored for far too long. Eugene had to find out who was responsible for the heroin distribution in the black communities. He knew that the President didn't know anything about black neighborhoods. Somebody was being used as a political puppet by the Sons of Liberty to push their dirt. It was his job to find out who that somebody was and terminate him.

Laura was officially in love with Tony. The two were inseparable, like ebony and ivory piano keys. She still managed to get a little politicking in between her torrid sexual sessions with her bodyguard. The twins liked Tony and anything was a step above the treatment that they witnessed their mom fall victim to from their late great father. Compared to him, Tony was a breath of fresh air. He respected and protected their mother, and as long as she was happy, they were happy. Ms. Bush had to slow things down a bit because now she was a political figure in the south. It was 2005, but there were still a lot of Georgians with racist attitudes. She really didn't care, but Tony had urged her to tone down their courtship. They had to be realistic about things.

Georgia was still a confederate state, but Senator Laura wanted to change the world. She was finally alone in her Atlanta mansion and she sat behind her designer desk. She was still a stickler for name brands. As she sat there, deep in thought, she wondered how she could use her new found power and authority to change the world. The possession of wealth was nothing without the ability to have a positive effect on society.

She thought back to the horrors of her life with George and thanked God that she no longer had to deal with the beatings or the mental abuse. Senator Bush felt free for the first time. A total freedom that had been denied for the majority of her adult life. It felt good not to be ridiculed with putdowns for George's amusement. It felt good not to have to worry about being called fat or stupid by her husband. The feeling was an emotion that she did not miss. It felt good to wake up in the morning and smile at the person she saw in the mirror. She was no longer vain and uncompromising. She no longer felt inferior or inadequate in her role as a strong independent woman. She was happy with the life she was living and had responsibilities for the first time in a very long time. She had grown so much since George had died and had come to be an excellent mother to her children. She wondered if she would have ever had an opportunity to become a senator as his wife. Those thoughts were quickly answered because she knew that it would have been impossible.

After a while, she became angry with herself for the person that she had become for money. She had compromised her soul for material wealth, but thankfully that past was far behind her. Now she had a new lease on life and was in control of her destiny. She was in a better position spiritually, emotionally and economically. She made her own decisions and lived by her own rules. The feeling of happiness showed in everything that she did and her heart was filled with joy. Senator Bush was on cloud ten.

Carl Watson had done his research. It had taken him several months to go through all of the information that Doug Winters had left in his office. It was enough information about Cheney Burrows to write a thick unauthorized autobiography. He had to go through each tidbit of information in detail because everything was a piece to a complete puzzle. It was as if Doug knew that his devotion to his cause was going to cost him his life. After reviewing the information, he knew why.

Carl had become so engulfed in carrying on Doug's story that it had magically became his story. The truth was now going to be revealed and his friend was not going to have died in vain. He spent very little time with his family and his social life was a thing of the past. He was obsessed with getting to the bottom of what the President had going on. He was going to find out why Doug Winters had been killed so tragically. He knew that Doug was on to something. Whatever it was, it had cost his friend his life. As he probed further into the methodical mess that Doug had left, he discovered the footage on Jim Irvin, the cowboy from Oklahoma. He had information about his disappearance and notes about how it was somehow related to the death of former President Bush. Nobody had questioned the President's death; the plane explosion had happened so long ago. From the looks of it, Cheney Burrows had something to do with it and there was a connection between Bush's death and the disappearance of the kid name Jim Irvin.

Mr. Watson was a skilled journalist and his journalistic hunches were usually correct. As he wrote down the information on Jim Irvin's parents, his instincts as a beat reporter came alive. He had a newfound passion for the game, a spark that lit his fire, a reason to take his research to the next two levels. Carl Watson was heading to Oklahoma because that was the site of his next big story.

Eugene L. Weems, Timothy R. Richardson

CHAPTER 17

Timothy swerved his fully stocked Cadillac Escalade through South Central Los Angeles traffic. He was running late for his 8:00 o'clock appointment with Lil' C, his established heroin connection. Agent Richardson had his mind on too many things that had nothing to do with surviving in the dog-eat-dog world of the California street life. He had brought a lot of attention to himself because he was the only connection that the street gangs had to the premium grade heroin that by now every addict in Southern California craved. His dashing good looks and smooth persona had earned him the street name, *Tip Toe*. His reputation was almost statewide, from Compton to Oakland.

As he continued his journey, his mind was filled with thoughts of Condoleeza. For some strange reason, he could not get her off his mind. The conversation that they had was still vivid in his mind. He had a strange feeling in the pit of his stomach that he could not shake. Timothy had never had such a feeling before and he knew that he was experiencing an emotion that was totally foreign. He was beginning to have a new outlook on the double life he was living. He was actually worried about Condoleeza's well being. It was something about the way she made him feel whenever he was in her presence. Sure, Timothy had more than his fair share of women and was still at the top of his game, but it was something special about the Vice President that touched his soul. Maybe it was the way she spoke to him in their many conversations about unlimited topics. Maybe it was the way he felt whenever he was in her presence. It was a feeling that made him feel important, as if he was needed. Timothy was feeling emotions for her that he did not think he was capable of expressing in a relationship. The problem was omnipresent. It was affecting his job. He was beginning to feel guilty about being used as a pawn by Director Prescott.

The glamour of being a street dealer had long since lost its attractiveness. The positives of street life were rapidly becoming negatives. He was beginning to have a heart, and a heart in his line of work could prove to be tragically dangerous. There was no way that he could ever show human emotion as a street dealer. His clientele were street thugs and known killers. Timothy had to display a certain persona in order to stay alive and he was losing his edge. He was losing that persona.

Timothy pulled up to the driveway of the rundown house of Lil' C. Several addicts were outside, wandering around like fiendish zombies. Timothy announced his presence, "What's up, where's Lil' C?" He had mastered the street lingo.

"He ain't here," a short, pudgy black man responded. Timothy didn't recognize him.

"What you want with Lil' C," an overly inquisitive loser responded. Obviously, something was seriously wrong and Timothy began to wonder about the situation. He had just talked to Lil' C moments ago and he knew all about the meeting, so he wondered about his tardiness.

Timothy was a very important person in the hood. He was the supplier and he held the lifeline to the heroin that was being distributed into the black community. He and Lil' C went way back to his days when he and Timothy played high school football at Compton's Centennial High School. Being late was not Lil' C's style, so Timothy decided to wait outside for a couple minutes. If he didn't show up, Timothy was going to make a few phone calls and then take his business elsewhere.

Timothy returned to his vehicle and began to think about his relationship with Condoleeza. As he sat alone in his vehicle, his mind began to wander, thinking about marriage for the very first time. Although he was really bugging out, he realized that he could have done a lot worse than marrying the Vice President of the United States. Ms. Kincaid stayed on his mind for some reason and he couldn't abandon thoughts of her. Unfortunately, he was in the wrong environment for thoughts about love. All of a sudden, he heard a tap at his car window. It was the short, pudgy guy from earlier. Timothy rolled down his window, the diamonds on his Rolex watch glistened in the moonlight.

"Hey, homey, got a light?" Timothy hated the interruption, but complied anyway. As he reached into his pocket, he noticed the other thug trying to open the passenger door of his vehicle. Suddenly, he felt the impact of a sharp pain on his temple. The gangster had punched him, catching Timothy off guard, but his natural instinct made him reach for his cannon. Timothy was too late because Mr. Uneducated had beat him to the draw and before long there were two guns to his one.

"Get yo' ass out that ca' muthafucka! This is a jack move."

Timothy knew better than to surrender, so he ducked and started the SUV in one fluid motion. Both guns exploded toward the vehicle simultaneously. Timothy had managed to throw the SUV in reverse and fired shots at the closest silhouette as he watched it fall to the ground. All of a sudden, he felt a burning sensation in his chest area and then another one in his shoulder. He had been hit twice. His pulse quickened as he pulled out the driveway in disbelief of what had occurred. The second attacker shot off several rounds at his retreating vehicle. Somehow, he managed to jump the curve and escape in one piece. He could not believe it. For the first time in his life, he had been shot. His adrenaline kept him focused as he made a detour to Martin Luther King Hospital. Timothy couldn't believe that he had been caught slipping. He should have known better than to have his mind on anything else besides his environment. A puddle of blood had gathered in the driver's seat of his Escalade. He thanked God for giving him the sense to wear his bullet proof vest.

After making it to the hospital's emergency room, Timothy quickly revealed his CIA credentials. He was thrown on the nearest cart and hauled off to the first available surgeon. Several thoughts circled through his mind as he was lying there, leaking blood. He thought about all the times he had peddled dope and made a profit from drug sales. He wondered if the chances he took daily, risking his life for Prescott, were really worth the price he was paying. Finally, he thought about Condoleeza and images of her beautiful face showed vividly in his head. His mind was full of thoughts of that beautiful face and he couldn't help but wonder if he was ever going to see her again.

The Sons of Liberty had their first meeting since President Burrows had been re-elected to the White House. All of the usual players were there; the President, CIA Director Prescott, Secretary of State Phil Rivers, and a new face, Texas governor Tex McClure.

"We have to vote on an issue that has been troubling our progress. Our administration has been troubled by the RNF for far too long. That is why we must bring the termination of Eugene Weems to a vote. All in favor, speak so accordingly."

"Aye," said Tex McClure.

"Aye," said CIA Director Prescott.

"Aye," said Phil Rivers.

"So it's unanimous. Director Prescott, do you have anyone in your organization capable or should we hire someone from the outside?"

"Sir, the CIA specializes in terminations. It won't be a problem," Prescott announced confidently.

"Well, we can't afford any screwups. Do not underestimate this animal. He has been known to retaliate. We still owe him one for Herman. I have a feeling that his organization was behind the death of my friend."

"Sir, failure is not in the CIA vocabulary. I will have my best men on it."

"Fine, then let's discuss another issue. How is Operation Cyclops going?"

"My men are doing fine work and we have surpassed $750 million profit." The CIA director was proud of his work.

"Good, that's all that I have for now. We will meet again. I will contact each one of you for our next conference. The same rule applies for departures. You will leave in 30-minute intervals. Is that understood?"

"Yes," the others said in unison.

Thirty minutes later, Director Prescott left in his limousine and headed west from Camp David. After 30 minutes, Governor McClure left and he headed east from their meeting site. Finally, the Secretary of State left and headed north. The President was alone and went through thoughts about his plot to control the world. He was actually more comfortable with being alone by himself these days. Money tends to have that effect on people. The President was richer than he had ever been in his life and had far more money than he had ever imagined. He had used the power of his position to perfection and he was virtually untouchable.

He still had the CIA under his control and the FBI was at his beck and call. He had several stash spots for the millions that he was making in the heroin trade. After being re-elected, he had a complete term to do his political magic and he was well on the verge of retiring a billionaire, even without a re-election. His plan was working out to perfection and operating on all cylinders. The American public didn't have a clue as to what was going on in the White House.

Once removed of his problem with Eugene Weems, he would no longer have the problem of the reparations bill. Hopefully, everything would work out this time. Mr. Weems was indeed a major force to be dealt with. The RNF was more and more difficult to label a terrorist organization. They had too many members and everybody knew of the President's dislike of their organization. He was still upset that they had managed to pull off the murder of his longtime friend, Herman Lee, and nobody was even indicted to stand trial.

The RNF was irritating the hell out of the President in a major way and he wanted life to be perfect. He had worked too hard to become powerful in his country. The only thing standing in his way from becoming omnipotent was the RNF. Getting rid of their organization and its purpose was becoming a major concern for him. Cheney wondered how information was being leaked from his organization to the mass media. He knew that leaks had to be coming from somewhere else in the White House. Thoughts began to circle through his mind of who that person was.

Ultimate power was his for the taking. He was like a pawn that had crossed over to the other side. He was the ruler of the most powerful country in the world. His life had meaning and he had respect. Now, all that he had to do was funnel his energies into concocting a master plan of destruction for the RNF. Eugene Weems had a loyal following that was in the millions, so he had to be careful. Once terminated, there would be a lot of attention focused on Cheney. He had to come up with a way to assassinate his character and turn Eugene's followers against him. It was a complex chess game that he was playing and all the political resources of the American government were on his side. It was only going to be a matter of time until he came up with the game-winning move.

George had developed a following among the white people in Acirema. Everyone wanted to meet the brilliant white man who dared to speak negatively about black people. It started with John and Penelope, then Penelope brought two of her friends and they brought along two friends. Before long, there were several people in and out of Penelope's house. At first, George wanted to keep a low profile, but eventually he realized that it was going to be impossible to remain anonymous.

He had found out so much about Caucasian Acireman culture from John and the scientist was like a walking encyclopedia of information on their history.

The white Aciremans had been denied the right to vote in Acirema elections until about 20 years prior to George's arrival. Even after the right to vote was granted, many black Acireman communities implemented factors like poll taxes and grandfather clause that stated, if your grandfather was not able to vote, you could not vote in the election. Sinister plots were concocted to prevent whites from voting. Many black Aciremans viewed white Aciremans as being too incompetent to participate in the democratic process. The powers that be had even passed a one-half compromise, whereby a white vote counts as half a black vote. In this bill, it took two white votes to equal one black vote. Since white Aciremans only made up about 15 percent of the Acirema population, their political influence was obsolete.

George became more and more in demand as a speaker and people would come from all over the township to hear him speak. He talked about moving the masses, the bullet or the ballot, liberty or death, and aroused action among the whites in Acirema. He believed that blacks would split equally on their choices for Acirema President and, although whites were in the minority, they could unify their vote and have an impact on the Presidential election. He used terms like *niggers, coons*, and other derogatory terms never heard before in reference to blacks. George had a radical way of thinking for a white man that was not seen in Acirema before. He was an Acireman hero, a man before his time. To white people, he was a living messiah and he was idolized by all.

Penelope had changed her view of this political warrior. She had actually fallen for his good looks and debonair ways. The fact that he had become the peach of every white woman's eye in Acirema didn't hurt either. Before long, their courtship had turned into a full blown relationship and the two became sexually intimate. They were a hot topic of conversation, the revolutionary and his mistress. They were the talk of the town.

Every now and then, George would be alone and think about getting home to America, but as each day passed, he came less and less confident about his ability to return there. He had made a decent life for himself in Acirema, but he still missed the luxuries of home. Somehow, he had to figure out a way to get back to his presidency. Things were still so horribly backwards in Acirema for him. He could never get used to life as he saw it there. However, he did relish his role as a leader and enjoyed the challenge of educating his followers. Maybe, in some strange and demented way, it was his destiny.

Even with all the newfound popularity, George was still a convicted felon on the run. Part of his mind was very untrusting and he feared going back to the horrors of the Acirema prison system. He still had nightmares about the months in the hole and how he would have to survive days without food. George did not want to return to those conditions. He was going to do everything in his power to remain a free man. Nothing could compare to the horrors of the prison life that he had experienced. The more that he thought about it, the more he wanted to leave Acirema forever.

Condoleeza had not slept in two days. Upon hearing the news that Timothy had been shot, she dropped everything that she was scheduled to attend in England and immediately returned to the United States. Finally, she arrived at the hospital and stood over a recovering Timothy.

"Don't you ever do that to me again. I didn't think you were going to make it." Condoleeza was crying, clutching Timothy's hand.

"Baby, it was only a couple of flesh wounds. Thank God I remembered to put on my vest." Timothy was trying to appear cool.

"What were you thinking, being in a neighborhood like that alone?"

"Well, it was part of my assignment. That's what I do for a living whenever I'm not being harassed by you."

"Well, get used to it because from now on you are permanently assigned to me and I'm not going to change one bit. I love you, Timothy, and I missed you."

"I...love you, too. I finally realized that when my life flashed before my eyes, but let's take things one day at a time."

Later on that night, Condoleeza was asleep in the chair at Timothy's bedside. Usually, the hospital did not allow overnight visitors, but they made an exception for the Vice President of the United States. She had a broad smile on her face that was wider than the Grand Canyon. Timothy had finally confessed his love to her and she felt complete for the very first time. She had a very special man in Mr. Richardson and was not going to let him go for the world. They were soul mates.

The Vice President was finally able to relax. Things were looking up. She traveled the world and spread democracy, and every now and then she would sit in on a house meeting. Condoleeza was gaining her own identity and separating herself from the President philosophically. Everyone knew about her support of the reparations movement, although Cheney opposed it outright. The old Condoleeza would have never showed opposition to the President. The old Condoleeza was a devout yes woman. Times change and she had changed. The new Ms. Kincaid had more confidence, and she owed it all to Timothy. Long gone were the days when she would smile around whites for no reason at all. Long gone were the moments when she was gullible and agreed with things just to fit in. Now she made the decisions. She was the one who did the judging and it felt good to be genuine for a change. The decision to support the reparations bill was not a popular one, but she was going to go with what she believed. Her decision to fall in love with her bodyguard was not in her best interest, but she ignored the negative thoughts. Now, if she was going to fail, it was going to be on her own terms.

The threats by President Burrows were challenged now. No more verbal abuse. She was not going to tolerate it. Everyone feared the President, but not Condoleeza. She knew who the real Cheney Burrows was and all the political power in the world was not going to change her opinion of him. Cheney was still the geek nerd with the thick glasses to her. She was not going to conform to his world anymore. She was not going to allow him to ridicule her thoughts or opinions anymore. Condoleeza was finally free and able to make her own rules.

It was not a position that was the most popular, but she was tired of being seen and not heard. The rumors of the past were far behind. She was no longer married to a man that she didn't love. The need of fitting in no longer suffocated her being, and she didn't mind if people did not like her. For the first time in her life, she was proud of who she was. Almost losing the man she loved gave her a different outlook on life. Now she felt capable with her role as Vice President. People looked at her in a different light and respected her more than before. She was a different person that demanded their respect. What others said about her didn't matter. She was secure in her position and nobody could call her incompetent without argument. She finally could look in the mirror and love what she saw, because Condoleeza was loved by Timothy Richardson.

Eugene Weems slammed his phone down in disgust. It was so hard to hire outsiders to do a job that Peaches could have done in her sleep. The two contracted buffoons had failed to kill the CIA conspirator that was spreading heroin all over California. Now the CIA knew that their plan was discovered and they would most definitely counter with a new heroin connect. Mr. Weems would have to start his job all over and await more information from his contacts in Washington, D.C. He found it hard to believe that out of 20 million following he could not find a good assassin. From now on, he was going to limit himself to Peaches and the Black Sphinx.

Eugene sat alone in his study and thought about his next move. So much had changed with one blunder, now Cheney had the upper hand. The leader of the RNF would now have to wait in hiding for Cheney's next move. The two powerful men were involved in a high stakes game of chess with real live people as the pieces. One wrong move could result in a loss of life. So far, there had been many casualties of war with two master strategists struggling for the advantage. The big picture was the reparations bill and the immediate focus was their egos. Neither man wanted to lose the war.

Things with the RNF were going well. Eugene had a worthy ally in Kendu Marley, his Vice President. The two shared similar philosophies for the progress of the RNF, but it was not the same as when he had Dr.

Phillips. Dr. Phillips was one of the few people that Eugene had looked up to in his complex life. Eugene missed him dearly and nobody could replace him, but the reparations movement had to go on. His speech in front of the United Nations had brought worldwide attention to the movement for reparations in America, but who was he kidding. Eugene realized that the politicians in America controlled the United Nations. They would never pass any worthwhile sanctions against the American government. So, in turn, real progress for the struggle fell on mute ears. The CIA propaganda machine had already had him labeled as a terrorist.

So much had been lost when his organization was denied the right to have the One million a Month rallies in Washington. Even Mr. Weems knew that the rallies could not last forever. Now he had to strategize his next move while his petitions were getting signed. He figured if he got all of his followers in America to sign a petition to bring the reparations bill to a vote, maybe it could be on the 2008 election ballot. Four more years was entirely too much time to have to wait. The President of the RNF did not want to have to wait that long; his people had already waited over 400 years.

He finished going over the final details of the meeting with Kendu Marley. The second phase of the One million a Month rally was going into effect. Since they had been banned from the White House lawn, he was going to move the monthly rally to the doorstep of the United Nations. Maybe the world would be a more willing audience than President Burrows. The RNF had millions of members abroad and eventually maybe some nation would drum up the courage to challenge the United States on the issue of slavery, considering America had always promoted itself as a leader in the civilized world for human rights.

It was a long day and the two men decided to break for the evening and continue the next day. Kendu Marley was no Dr. David Phillips, but he definitely was a loyal and able Vice President for the RNF organization.

"Sir, things should work out with the Million a Month march. New York should prove to be a worthy location indeed."

"Yes, Mr. Marley, it was an excellent suggestion on your behalf. What are your plans for the evening?" Eugene was in rare form and actually was in a good mood.

"Well, it's my wife's birthday. She's been waiting patiently for me at home all day. I'm going to treat her to a dinner and maybe a play downtown Chicago."

"That's sounds good. It's Naomi's birthday? Why don't you take her out in class for a change. Here, take my Rolls Royce." Eugene tossed his comrade the car keys.

"Sir, I can't possibly take your vehicle. What if something happens to your car?"

"No problem, don't worry, I have top flight insurance. I'm covered. Go ahead, enjoy yourselves. The two of you deserve it." Eugene was insistent.

"Okay, sir, if you insist. I will be extra careful."

The worrisome Marley exited the office of Eugene's estate a bit happier because his wife was going to love the Rolls Royce. It was a dream car that any woman would love, even though Naomi wasn't materialistic in any kind of way.

Eugene sat back at his desk, feeling good about having performed a good deed for his hardworking comrade. He was faced with the foreign situation of not having anything to do for the evening, so he gave Peaches a call on her private line. She answered in one ring.

"Peaches?"

"Yes, your Excellency."

"I am in need of comfort tonight."

"Of course, sir, I will be there shortly."

"Bring wine and wear something sexy."

"Can I be anything else but sexy to you?"

"Of course not. See you."

The leader of the RNF hung up the phone, visualizing the treat that Peaches had in store for him. He sat back in his leather seat behind his desk. Only a few moments had gone by since his comrade, Marley's departure. Out of nowhere there was an enormous explosion that rocked the very foundation of Eugene's estate. The first thing that came to mind was his Rolls Royce and Kendu Marley. Eugene immediately sensed that something was wrong. He rushed outside to his driveway and all he saw were the remnants of his vehicle. It was a car bomb and there was no doubt who it was intended for, but unfortunately for Mr. Marley, the wrong person had started the luxury vehicle.

Eugene stood in disbelief, wondering how he had been caught off guard at his own home. He should have known better than to leave his vehicle unattended. Now his friend was dead. There was no question as to who was responsible for the act. The only reaction he had was to plan his revenge. He immediately got his private cell phone, "Peaches."

"Yes, Your Excellency."

"There's been a slight change in plans. Mr. Marley is no more. I still want you to come by, but it's strictly business now."

"Fine, sir, I understand." They hung up simultaneously.

Eugene Weems stood alone. Now he had to find a way to explain the madness of the accident to Kendu Marley's wife. He hated accidents and he hated explaining the death of one of his warriors even more. Anger soon replaced the emotion of loss. They had successfully awakened the spirit of a warrior. The leader of the RNF would have to be very careful and plan his retaliation in secret. President Burrows had the power of the entire American government behind him. He was still too risky a target, but Eugene wanted him to pay. He wanted him to feel the pain of loss, and it was going to have to be a major loss.

He said goodbye to Kendu Marley and praised him as another brother fallen for the cause. He soon realized how easily it could have been him in that vehicle, and

224

then realized how precious life was. He then made two phone calls. First, he called Carl Watson at the *Chicago Tribune* and told him about the plot to take his life. He wanted to bring attention to his plight and to ensure that Kendu Marley received a proper send-off in the papers. Second, he made the difficult call to Mrs. Marley and explained to her that her husband would not be home for her birthday.

Laura was doing an excellent job as a Georgia senator. Her performance was outstanding and she had surprised even herself with how smoothly her transition into the world of politics had gone. It felt good to be able to stand on her own two feet without constraints. The political world enabled her to have power in decision-making for millions of Georgians. It was a feeling of responsibility that she enjoyed. She would go to Washington, D.C. every now and then for meetings of Congress, but her visits nowadays took on a completely different meaning than before when she was the First Lady. Now that she had a difficult role as a leader, Washington was no longer a burden. It was almost a beautiful site.

The children enjoyed having a mother who was senator. They actually bragged about their mother and how she would travel all over the State of Georgia addressing the concerns of the citizens. Barbara respected her mom and their relationship had improved tenfold. She was far more outspoken and even protective of Laura. Jenna was turning out to be a smaller version of her mother. Even at her early age, she was very pretty. She, too, had learned to appreciate her mother more and wanted to become a senator herself.

Laura and Tony had done a good job of keeping their relationship a secret, but Laura was becoming frustrated with the secrecy. She wanted to bring their relationship to the forefront, but she realized it was a political risk to do so. Georgia was still a southern state and not too many people would approve of a Georgian senator involved in an interracial relationship. The state was still backwards in a lot of ways. Some people even assumed that she was still married to George Bush. She had, however, become very determined to stick to what she believed. She wanted the world to know about her love for her man. To her, it really did not matter what color he was. She was in love with Tony Gibson and she didn't care who knew, but she had to be realistic; announcing their relationship could be political suicide. Somehow, she was going to find a way to reveal her feelings, but it was still too soon. The timing just wasn't right, so for now she would have to live a secret double life, but she was determined to eventually reveal her true feelings, regardless of the consequences.

CHAPTER 18

Carl Watson discovered so much from his meeting with Mr. and Mrs. Irvin that he had reporter goose bumps. He could not wait to get back to his newspaper and bring his article to print. He had uncovered a big story and realized that Doug Winters was on to a story that was going to turn Washington, D.C. inside out. He was really on to something and now he knew why Doug had been murdered. Now he had the challenge of figuring out a way to bring the story of Jim Irvin's disappearance to the American public. He did not want to hit them with too much information at once. He had already released the story about Kendu Marley and implicated the CIA for his death. The editor in chief had received several threats from the government with sanctions against his paper. It was obvious to him that the powers that be in Washington were trying to silence him. They were on to him, but Carl was a proven veteran, a journalistic fox, and he was not about to wear his emotions on his sleeve for the entire nation to see.

He was going to plot his next move in secrecy. Too much was at stake.

His journalistic senses were boiling and he felt an excitement that he remembered from his early days as a beat reporter. He knew that somebody in Washington had caused Jim Irvin to disappear, but the question was who and why. He also knew that it had something to do with former President George Bush, but he could not make the connection between the two men. Even with his journalistic power, he realized that he could not afford to print the wrong story to the public, so he would have to do his research and figure out the truth out of the mess that Doug had left for him. There were a lot of questions and he had to find some answers. He had his work cut out for him. He could see why Doug had become so engulfed in the story to begin with. It was Pulitzer Prize winning journalism in the making. It was a major story that was going to take his career to a higher level. Now, it was all left up to Carl to deliver his friend's story to the world, but first he had some questions for a Georgia senator.

Timothy Richardson had fully recovered from his bullet wounds and, to his delight, was reunited with Condoleeza Kincaid. He had a new lease on life, which gave him a new perspective. He could not believe that he had been shot trying to peddle drugs for the CIA. He had to make a decision about his career. His attraction to Condoleeza was at an all time high, and he had never felt that way about a female before. Could this be love?

Director Prescott had taken the news of Timothy's attempted murder in anger. Although he felt bad for Timothy, he was more disappointed that the flow of heroin had been interrupted. Timothy could tell from the tone of his voice that he did not care about Timothy's welfare one way or the other. It was crystal clear where his priorities were, and they were not with Agent Timothy Richardson.

Timothy was becoming more and more disgruntled with his position in the CIA. He wanted a calmer life in the background and out of the fast lane. Things were too hostile on the streets and he had already experienced just about everything that he could have imagined. He had seen the view from the top of the game: the money, the cars, the jewelry, and the countless women. He had seen the lows: the dope fiends, the arrests, and now even having his life flash before his eyes. Now he wanted a calmer environment, something more stable, something out of the limelight with a slower pace. Make-up sex with Condoleeza was intense and had made his toes curl. He hoped that he wasn't blowing things out of perspective, but this time around things seemed different between them. The connection stronger, the intensity heightened. He was through with the games and playing guinea pig for the CIA and Director Prescott. His loyalties were different now and he had a newfound commitment to Ms. Kincaid. She was the only person who truly cared about him, the only person who came to visit him in the hospital. He could not go along with living a lie anymore and now he had to tell her the truth.

"Condoleeza, I have something that I need to discuss with you." Timothy wanted her undivided attention.

"Yes, Timothy, what is it? Don't scare me like that. You look so serious."

"I'm serious. Baby, there's something I have to tell you."

"What is it, Timothy, I'm listening."

After a brief pause, Timothy finally got up the nerve to speak the truth. "My assignment. At first, I was put here as an informant, a mere spy to report every move that you made."

"A what! What are you talking about? I can't believe it." His honesty took Condoleeza by surprise.

"Leeza, Leeza, please let me finish."

"Please, do. You have some serious explaining to do."

"When I was in the hospital, almost murdered for a cause I didn't believe in, you were there for me. You came through and helped me make it out alive. I appreciated that, and it was at that time that I realized how wrong I was. I couldn't continue the lie anymore."

"Is that why you decided not to marry me?"

"Yes. I felt like I didn't deserve a woman like you. You are beautiful, honest, smart, loving, and the woman of my dreams."

"Well, how could you spy on the woman of your dreams?"

"My point exactly. Let's start over. Let's make things right between us. I'm sorry. Let's start off by being friends again with no lies. I promise, no more lies."

Condoleeza was quiet for a moment, then she responded. "I don't know, Timothy, our entire relationship was built on lies. I have to think about it. Please, leave." Condoleeza went over and opened the door. Timothy said nothing else. He just got his jacket and departed. He knew that he was taking a risk by telling her the truth, but it was a risk worth taking for his peace of mind.

Condoleeza was alone and wondered if she had made the right decision. She knew that Timothy was just doing what he had been ordered to do, but somehow that was not enough. She felt betrayed and used. Once again, she had put her faith in a man, in a relationship, and she had been fooled. She was angry with herself for trusting love.

George was getting used to his role as a leader in Acirema. His confidence had again risen to the level of conceit. Many of the whites in Acirema were uneducated. John was one of the few whites that had graduated from college at one of the all whites universities. It was obvious that the black educational system was far better than the white. This made it very easy for George to manipulate his followers. During his speeches, he would use big words that were difficult to understand. Many whites would come from all around to hear him speak. He had no equal and was the envy of the white men in Acirema. He was still handsome for his age and the women loved him. Penelope had her hands full trying to fend off the groupies.

Life was better for him, but it still was not home. George felt like a ship lost at sea. No matter how comfortable he got in Acirema, he would always feel like a visitor. Late at night, he would have dreams of escaping through the other side of the mirror and returning home to America. He had a newfound appreciation for his freedom. He had learned his lesson and was not going to take his family for granted again. If only he could figure out a plan to get back to the estate of President Barack Obama. He relished his role as a leader, but from time to time he still wanted to get back to life as he once knew it. Sometimes, George would get an empty feeling deep in the pit of his stomach and wish that his nightmare would end. Although he should have been happy with his role as messiah, nothing was like being President of the United States of America.

Days and nights went by slowly, as if time were standing still. His memories of life at home made him realize that he had taken so much for granted. Never again would he abuse his wife or beat his children for no apparent reason. Never again would he take his freedom for granted or carelessly disregard the views of others. George had struggled, but he had learned from his struggle that his life was a piece of cake compared to what whites in Acirema had to face, which was so similar to what blacks on Earth in America had lived with for hundreds of years.

Despite his struggles, he had deep hatred for everything that was black. Although he had more respect for the blacks in Acirema, his hatred of what they stood for was great. He viewed them as racist and saw them as oppressors of his people. It was a cold game that they played with the lives of his white brothers and sisters, a game that was unfair, where they had the disadvantage. It was like trying to play tennis with your hands tied behind your back.

Acirema was a land that was like a prison and George wanted out. He wanted to be in the majority for a change. He wanted to be the favorite and not the underdog. He wanted his life back as a white, wealthy billionaire in America. He would go to sleep each night and dream about life on the other side of the mirror and wake up to the reality of Acirema. He was going to do whatever it took to make things right. He and John stayed up late at night perfecting their plans to infiltrate the President's mansion. George was going to get back home by any means necessary.

The leader of the Sons of Liberty sat behind the desk in his Oval Office. So much had changed for Cheney Burrows. His love affair with his American public was so fickle. It was love one day and hate the next. These days, it was more of the latter due to the accusations that his administration was responsible for the car bomb that took the life of RNF Vice President Kendu Marley. Almost everyone knew of the President's hatred of the RNF, and many people felt that the car bomb was intended for Eugene Weems. The nation was in an uproar and he had awakened a sleeping giant with just one miscalculation. Now he had to figure a way to make up for the CIA blunder. The RNF had followers well into the millions and they started their Million a Month rallies in front of the United Nations. Something had to be done. It was going to take all of his political power to stop the marches in New York. His political power didn't reach as far as it used to and New York was a liberal state. The RNF was at full steam in that area and it was going to take all of his influence to stop the rallies there.

His personal life was also suffering and he was at the point where he was fed up with Marry Ann. She had become a burden, especially after Director Prescott told him about her visits at Norma's beauty salon. To his surprise, his wife didn't see anything wrong with revealing secrets of what was going on in the White House to complete strangers. Finally, he had lifted his right hand and slapped her back to reality, a slap that may have caused him his marriage. Mary Ann had moved out of the White House and back to Indiana with her parents. To think that he thought the leak was an infiltrator and the entire time it was coming from sex talk with his gossiping wife.

The heroin trade was stagnant to say the least. After losing his distributor to a failed assassination attempt by

the RNF, things were slow.   He had put additional
pressure on Director Prescott to have someone replace
Timothy, but his replacement was not as suitable.   The
assassination attempt had the African American members
of the CIA hesitant to accept the position. They all had
heard about the agent who held the post. None of them
wanted to challenge the RNF. They were too powerful.

Cheney sat back, wondering what George would have
done in this situation. The RNF was a fucking nuisance
that was causing problems for him on all fronts. He had
to figure out a way to get rid of them. He knew that
Mary Ann had leaked information, but he assumed that
someone else was dealing with the RNF, somebody from
the inside, because they always seemed to have the upper
hand on the inside dealings of his administration. He
was determined to find out who was the source, and once
he found out who it was, he was going to deal with them
the CIA way.

For now, he had to control things that he could. His
wife had already talked to the media about their marital
problems. The President was forced to make a decision
by his peers in the Sons of Liberty. He was already
viewed as a failure in his relationship and now he was
losing the respect of his followers. Something had to be
done now to silence that big-mouth bitch, Mary Ann. He
viewed himself as above her and was tired of their
relationship. He made up his mind. He was not going to
make the mistake of depending on the misfits at the CIA
to handle this task for him.   He was going to silence

Mary Ann on his own. He was going to silence her forever.

CHAPTER 19

Condoleeza Kincaid was nervous beyond belief. She had been experiencing morning sickness for the past several days. Something was horribly wrong with her system. She feared the worst. It had been a few weeks since she had last talked to Timothy, although he was constantly on her mind. Now she thought about him even more than ever.

She thought back on the day that she showed him the door out of her life for the second time. She wondered if she had made the right decision. Her life was basically in shambles and now this sickness had overcome her. Without her protector, she felt insecure, and without her lover, she felt lonely. She realized that Timothy did not have control over the CIA powers that be, and that Cheney was behind the scheme to spy on her life, but that did not take away from the feeling of betrayal that she felt. Timothy should have let her know of his intentions sooner. He should have revealed the truth sooner. Still, he had finally come forward with the truth, knowing the risk he took of losing her again.

So much went through this troubled black woman's mind as she stared at herself in the mirror. She thought back to how she felt when she first found out that Timothy had been shot. She then thought back to how she felt when she found out about the betrayal. Her life with Timothy was bittersweet, but she had to admit that it was mostly sweet. Now she had to deal with this new situation.

Her stomach was tied in knots as she impatiently awaited the results of the home pregnancy test. So much as at risk with the results of a simple two-minute test. It was the longest two minutes of her life, so much was at stake. Ms. Kincaid first had been through so many different scenarios in life, but being a mother wasn't one of them. As she stared at the plus sign that magically appeared on the test wand, her mind finally accepted the truth of what her body had known for weeks. She was definitely pregnant.

Eugene Weems was fuming and wanted his revenge. His comrade received a hero's send-off, but nothing could relieve the sadness in the eyes of his widow. Mr. Weems had been met with adversity on several occasions. and this was one of the hardest times to stomach. It was obvious that the car bomb that took his ally's life was definitely intended for him. He would gladly have accepted his fate and died in his Vice President's place. Eugene was no coward. God was on his side, and, fortunately, he would live to fight another day. Hate was too weak a word to describe the emotion that he felt for the President. Two of his closest friends had been lost in the battle for the cause, but he could not let his emotions overpower his keen intelligence. There was still a war to fight for his people and the enemy was not going to be able to savor this victory. As the final remains of Kendu Marley were put to rest, Eugene plotted his revenge. His next strike had to be a deadly one. He was tired of the silly games. It was his move now and he was going to make it count. The RNF was not going to be attacked without response. It was time for action.

In Houston, Texas, a well stuffed Tex McClure was being entertained by a stripper at Club Lipstick. He eventually departed with his bodyguards around him. It had all the accolades of a country and western star posse. He entered the confines of his limo without incident. A small crowd had gathered around to witness a hometown hero. He was handed a gift from one of his adoring fans. Tex didn't pay it any mind. He just tossed it in the back with the others. He was used to southern hospitality. With all of his wealth, he could not turn down a free present.

Pleasantly intoxicated, the entourage pulled out of the parking lot. The lone black female separated herself from the crowd. She pressed a button on a small device and another Son of Liberty was blown away. Needless to say, that was the last political gift that Tex McClure was going to receive.

Eugene received a phone call, "It's done," the sweet voice explained.

"Yes." No more words were spoken between the two individuals. No more words needed to be said. A rare smile graced the face of Mr. Weems. He quickly remembered where he was and got back into the funeral proceedings for his fallen Vice President. The warrior knew that there was no time to celebrate and his move was only a temporary victory. Besides, he had bigger fish to fry and it was only going to be a matter of time before his kitchen got hot.

President Burrows relaxed in the comfort of Camp David with his wife, Mary Ann. The two of them had just engaged in a brief sexual encounter and a long conversation about current events in the White House. He had enthusiastically told his wife all about the Sons of Liberty and Operation Cyclops. He had also told her the truth about the car bomb and how it was meant for Eugene Weems. Mary Ann was refueled with enough information to return to her weekly gossip sessions at Norma's, but Cheney had something else in mind.

He prepared the cocktails for the both of them in the privacy of the kitchen. He emptied the contents of two capsules into Mary Ann's drink. He stirred the contents and delivered the glass to his unsuspecting wife. He proposed a toast, "To loose lips. They sink ships, but our relationship has stood the test of time. May Mary Ann Wednesday become a thing of the past." Cheney's intent was evident as the two glasses touched each other.

"What do you mean by that?" Mary Ann had a confused look on her face. For once, Cheney didn't have an answer for the First Lady. He just ignored her words as the two drank their cocktails and engaged in conversation about unrelated topics. The rest of the evening went on without incident. Mary Ann had even moved all of her belongings back into the White House.

The following day, while Mary Ann was in the restroom preparing her makeup, she felt a sharp pain in her chest area. Shortly, the pain overwhelmed her entire body. It was a severe heart attack, courtesy of the CIA. Mary Ann was dead in a matter of minutes. Cheney was at the golf course with his pal, Director Prescott. The whole episode had been plotted to perfection.

Cheney received a phone call from the Secret Service, "Sir, it's the First Lady, she has had a heart attack." The White House security chief was at a loss of words.

"What do you mean, not my Mary Ann?" The President was a skilled actor.

"I'm afraid she is dead, sir." Hopelessness in his voice.

"What! I'm on my way." Cheney almost sounded genuine.

The President hung up the phone and then reached in the pocket of his jacket and retrieved two large Cuban cigars. He handed one to his partner in crime and lit both of them, "A toast to no more Marry Ann big mouth."

"I'll smoke to that," the director replied.

The two men took their time and finished their round of golf as if nothing had happened. Later, they received a second phone call.

"Sir, it's about Texas Governor McClure. He's dead. A car explosion." Cheney could not believe his ears and was outraged.

"What are you saying? Where were his bodyguards? How did this happen?" There was silence on the line from the victimized Secret Service Agent. The questions from an unbelieving President continued until finally he hung up the phone.

"They got Tex." The President was sad.

"What do you mean?" The CIA Director couldn't believe it either. Somebody had some explaining to do. Two deaths in one day was a lot of activity for even the Sons of Liberty.

Carl Watson had finally been granted an interview with Senator Laura Bush. One thing was certain; the editor in chief of a major newspaper had far more pull than a beat reporter. The two began their conversation on the record.

"Good afternoon, Mrs. Laura Bush, Senator for the State of Georgia. This is Carl Watson, Editor in Chief, *Chicago Tribune*." Carl was formal, the only way to get things accomplished with these types.

"Hello, Mr. Watson. It's a pleasure meeting you. I've heard about your paper and your reputation." Laura couldn't help but assume the professionally serious tone that was presented by the editor.

"Let's start with your election to the senate. Congratulations on being elected Georgia's senator. How are things going?" Carl got right down to business.

"Well, things are going wonderfully. As you can see, I have settled into my mansion, my two wonderful children are doing well, and things are peachy in Georgia." Simple enough, Laura had answered that question a million times.

"Many people want to know why you kept your married name when you ran for your seat in the senate instead of returning to your maiden name?" Carl was a journalistic fox. He quickly changed the tone of the interview.

"Well, I have never been asked that question. I kept my last name because I earned that right." Laura immediately took a defensive stance.

"How did your husband's disappearance play into your decision to enter into politics?" Things were starting to heat up. Laura was hearing the word *disappearance* for the first time in reference to her husband.

"Well, my husband's *death* had nothing at all to do with my decision to enter the world of politics. It was a decision that I obviously made on my own. I love the State of Georgia. It is my home and I wanted to make a difference." Laura was very serious by now. She did not like the direction that the interview was headed.

"Why did you leave the Washington, D.C. area?" Another question about the past that she wanted to forget.

"I left the Washington, D.C. area because I wanted to leave my experiences there behind me. I wanted to move closer to my roots, closer to my home."

"How did you come to the decision to leave Washington, D.C. behind you and decide later to run for senator? I'm confused." Carl had her on the ropes and prepared for the journalistic knockdown.

"I don't have to answer that question."

"Well, how about this one. How did your Texas mansion catch on fire?" A blow below the belt.

"I have no idea."

"We all know about your children, Barbara and Jenna. How did your move to politics affect them?" Finally, a question that she could answer, beauty contestant material.

"Well, the twins love our new home in Georgia. They have adjusted very well to their new environment." Laura enjoyed the brief break from the pressing questions.

"How did President Burrows feel about your move to Georgia?"

"I do not communicate with Cheney. That was a friend of George's. He and I were not that close. I suggest you set up an interview with him for that question." Laura was growing tired.

"Have you heard of the Sons of Liberty?" Carl moved in for the kill.

"The Sons of what? I don't know what you're talking about."

"Who is Jim Irvin from Oklahoma?" The kill was made.

"I have no idea."

"Where is your husband, George Walker Bush?" Salt to the wound.

"I have no idea what you're talking about. My husband died in a plane explosion. I'm offended that you asked that question of me. Mr. Watson, I believe that our interview is over. Your time is up." Laura was fed up.

"Tony, remove this man from my presence." Carl was quickly escorted out of the Georgia mansion and to his awaiting vehicle. Carl had been put out of far better establishments in his journalistic life.

Laura sat there, alone and in tears. Mr. Watson had opened several wounds from the past that were almost healed. She now realized how far she had progressed from her life with George Bush. Even with her newfound persona of confidence, she still feared returning to the life that she once lived. The queen of Bush Industries had come a very long way. It was a memory that she wanted closed forever, but there were still so many questions left unanswered. Who were the Sons of Liberty? Did Cheney Burrows fake the death of her husband? If so, where was the real George Bush? She sat there and pondered the questions over and over

245

again until she had a throbbing headache. As hard as she tried, she still could not come up with the answers, but she knew that they were out there somewhere. Her life had retreated to chaos again in a matter of minutes. She was not going to rest until she got the answers, and the only person who could answer her questions lived in the White House.

Carl Watson had hit a journalistic homerun. He loved to create drama, especially to the life of a rich and beautiful senator. He had been around the track several times and he realized that either Laura was an academy award winning actress or she had no clue as to what had happened to former President Bush. He would have bet his small fortune on the latter. Her responses were too spontaneous. Perpetrators didn't usually react in the fashion that she did. He could safely remove her as a player in the high stakes political game that was obviously going on.

Somebody had faked the death of the former President of the United States, but why? Who were the players in this game? Carl had a good idea that Cheney was behind it, but why would he kill his meal ticket? It was too complex a scheme for even Cheney to pull off by himself. Somebody very powerful in the government had helped him with his plot and Carl was going to find out who it was.

He was one step closer to figuring out the puzzle that had cost his friend, Doug, his life. Now he had to figure out a way to get to the bottom of what was going on in Washington, D.C. He had to get to President Burrows, but security was tighter than a mini skirt on a two-dollar hooker. The only other option was to bring the powers that be to Chicago. Carl probed his mind for his next course of action. He had to regroup and gather his thoughts. He was getting closer to the answers and he could not afford to get too careless. Whoever killed George Bush had put together a perfect plan, and to discover him, Carl's plan had to be flawless.

Timothy Richardson was totally confused. He was in love with Condoleeza, there was no doubt in his mind about that, but he was tired of their on-today/off-tomorrow relationship. The last conversation between the two of them had him in an uproar as he gathered himself for the face-to-face confrontation with the beautiful object of his desire.

"Timothy, I'm sorry for the way I have been acting toward you." Condoleeza began with an apology to her lover.

"Condoleeza, we can't go on like this. It's driving me crazy." Timothy confessed his feelings for the second time.

"I just have one more thing to say and you can make the decision to deal with me if you choose." Condoleeza had his attention.

"What could it possibly be this time? Are you going to put me out again? I'm tired of this shit. I'm tired of the games. What is it, Leeza? What could it possibly be that made you call me to come all the way back to

Washington?" Timothy was irritated and had reached the end of his endurance.

"Timothy, honey, I'm pregnant."

Timothy became dizzy and almost passed out in the very spot that he was standing. "Pregnant, I can't believe it!" He approached Condoleeza and compassionately embraced her in his arms. He was delighted, after the initial shock had worn off. "I love you, Condoleeza, God knows I do. Let's get married."

"Yes, Timothy, yes!" The two love birds engaged in a tongue lashing kiss that seemed to last for hours. Make-up sex was the welcome dessert.

Condoleeza was awake and lay next to her sleeping, satisfied lover. She was finally happy. She had a wonderful man in Timothy Richardson. She had a very promising career as Vice President of the United States. She was satisfied with who she was for the very first time in a long time. Life was looking good for the soon-to-be Condoleeza Richardson.

"I want his head on a platter! I want him dead right now, the fucking nigger!" Cheney was mad beyond belief.

"Sir, we can't tie him to the Tex McClure assassination. He had the perfect alibi. He was in Chicago at Kendu Marley's funeral proceedings."

"Who cares, he gave the order! I'm tired of excuses. I have enough problems of my own trying to deal with the death of my wife. The news media has been having a field day with my personal life."

"I understand, sir. I have agents working around the clock."

"Just get it done, and I mean now! I want that nigger dead, a barbed wire noose around his neck, his head severed, dead as a door nail, you understand!"

Cheney hit the end button on the cell phone in the palm of his hand. He did not take the news of the death of his longtime friend Tex McClure too well. His world was falling apart before his eyes. He sat in the confines of the Oval Office, frustrated beyond belief, sipping on fine Jack Daniels. Being President was not all that it was cut out to be and the mood in the White House was gray. President Burrows had seen better days. He poured another glass of Jack and thought about his next move as he watched the television in privacy. The next thing he saw took his depression to another level. It was Eugene Weems and Carl Watson on CNN. They were together on national television being interviewed by Larry King. They revealed everything: the death of Jim Irvin, the murder of Dr. David Lee Phillips, the Sons of Liberty and the conspiracy to distributed heroin throughout the black community, the cover-up of the disappearance of George Bush, the assassination attempt on the life of Eugene Weems, the death of Kendu Marley. They had recorded conversations, they had video footage, and it was all being played to a national audience.

He could not believe his eyes when he saw who the RNF infiltrator to the White House was. It was the White House butler. Old, faithful Benson had been a member of the RNF the entire time. The entire Oval Office had been bugged and the most secret conversations of the Sons of Liberty had been recorded. Somebody was watching the watchers.

Cheney immediately locked the doors of the Oval Office. He propped a chair against the doorknob for good measure. Almost immediately there were special agents knocking at his door and there was no doubt about their intentions. Cheney had abused his power as President. He was responsible for the deaths of many people. He had played a political chess game with Eugene Weems and had found himself in checkmate.

Cheney sat behind his desk, pleasantly intoxicated. He was not going to spend the rest of his life behind bars. Numbly, he reached in the desk drawer for his .45 magnum, put the muzzle in his mouth and blew his brains all over the American flag that hung behind him.

Condoleeza Richardson stood on the lawn of the White House, a proud mother to be, as her husband, the first gentleman, looked on. She accepted her post with pride. It was weird how things had changed so fast. Not too long ago, she was an unhappy wife and news anchor in Chicago. Worse things have happened in America politics. Actors have become governors, thieves have become Presidents. Today was the dawn of a new era. It was a joyous occasion. The world had been shocked when she selected Eugene Weems as her Secretary of State. It was a cabinet she would be proud of. The world looked on as the hometown sister accepted the Presidency of the United States. Condoleeza cried tears of joy. It was another first in a long line of firsts for her. She could not believe it as she was sworn in by the Chief Justice of the Supreme Court. Condoleeza Richardson was the first African American female and pregnant President of the United States.

George could not believe his fate as they strapped him into the chair for his execution. The attempt to make it home was a total failure. John was killed, along with many others that included eleven Acirema security personnel. As the sole survivor, George was charged with all of the deaths. Thus, he was sentenced to the death penalty for his crime of invading the Black House. So much had gone wrong in such a short amount of time. He made his final prayers to whatever Gods there may be. He had fucked up big time and now he was about to pay the price. He missed his family in America. He missed his longtime friend, Cheney Burrows, but most of all he missed being in power. It was all about to end for him with the pull of a switch. The black warden gave the order, "Pull."

There was a light. George awoke from a horrible nightmare. It was all a dream, he thought. What George would never know, is that the solar system had aligned, just as John had described, and just in the Nick of time. George checked himself to make sure that everything was okay. He was at his office in the White House. He got on his knees and thanked God. He immediately went over to his desk and took out his copy of the reparations bill and signed it. George had a change of heart for the very first time about the way he felt deep within about black people. They are human beings with emotions and rights, and entitled to be treated equally and with respect like any other human being. He glanced over at his reflection in his vanity mirror, and for the first time he liked what he saw.

He then grabbed a golf club from a golf bag and shattered the mirror into a million pieces, relieved to be back on earth, in America, in the comfort and familiarity of his office. He sank into the plush soft leather chair behind the desk and linked his fingers behind his head as he basked in the glory of his survival and return to the presidency.

He reached for the family portrait that he kept on his desk, and then froze in a state of shock. This was a reality he was reluctant to accept. He seized the picture frame and furiously launched it across the room in a rage of confusion. Then he reached for something else to throw, the nameplate that sat at the front of the desk. Just before he could hurl it across the room, he noticed the inscription, which read, *44th President of the United States of America, Barack Obama.*

"What the hell!" His mind was racing beyond light speed, trying to put together what could have happened.

It dawned on him that he had not returned to his Texas estate, where this paranormal experience began.   He turned to the shattered mirror, feeling overwhelmed with disgust and fear at what he had just done. Falling to his knees, he tried to gather the broken pieces of what he believed to be the only means of returning to his life.

George Bush was so consumed in his regret and fear, he wasn't even aware of the Secret Service men surrounding him, weapons drawn.   As he was being detained face-down on the carpet and put in handcuffs, he turned his face toward the Oval Office doorway. Immediately, he understood that the dashing figure of a man he saw standing there was the same man depicted in the family photo he had thrown across the room, the man known as the President of Acirema. *So how could it also be that he has become the 44th President of the United States of America?* George asks himself, as he is being hauled from the Oval Office...

THE END

Eugene L. Weems, Timothy R. Richardson

Sneak Peek Preview
INNOCENT
BY
CIRCUMSTANCE

Eugene L. Weems

Eugene L. Weems, Timothy R. Richardson

CHAPTER 1

This is what happened.

At the age of fifteen, my life began to undertake a dramatic twist, like an unexpected scene in a mystery novel. I could actually feel the strength of my demise, violently tugging at my soul and my physical being and the vital spirit of the godly ways that had been instilled in me since infancy.

When I was at the tender age of five, my mother had been killed in an automobile accident. I have only vague recollection of her physical presence, and fewer actual memories of childhood events that include her. I can't recall my sadness at her loss. I doubt that I recognized the actuality of the circumstances at the time. I don't even recall what she looked like. I made inquiries about her for several years, but as time passed, so did my curiosity.

My grandmother stepped into the role, and she upheld that title and responsibility unconditionally. She had been all that I cherished, the solid foundation to my basic morals and the shield that protected me from the sinful ways of the streets. She was beautiful in her effervescence. A person with a loving heart, caring personality, full of warmth, laughter and softness. She was extremely intelligent. I always felt she knew the answers to my questions and could easily solve all my problems. The big pearly white smile she constantly wore was more alluring and warming to a person's soul than the rays of the sun itself.

I was torn from my lovely black grandmother when she suffered cardiovascular trauma and went to an early grave. The doctor said she had bronchitis and emphysema, and her lungs collapsed from continuous years of cigarette smoking. I promised myself then that I would never indulge.

The day of her death was also the day of my death to the life that I cherished. Then began my quest for survival in the fast-paced treacherous and wicked streets of Las Vegas, Nevada. The ghettos, the hustling, larceny, robberies and burglaries committed just to maintain the necessities of life.

I had run away from the constant quarreling of family members who couldn't agree on my guardianship. It seemed they cared little for my welfare, but only about which of them would oversee the funds left in trust for me in my grandmother's life insurance, of which I had been designated sole beneficiary. I cared little about the money, because it could never ease the pain of her loss.

So I emptied my leather backpack of school materials, then stuffed a small lightweight blue blanket inside, along with my pet ferret, Squeegee, and a few of his things. I pocketed the loose change that was scattered atop my dresser and took one last inventory of the items I had gathered for the journey, realizing that I had forgotten Squeege's ferret snacks. When I was satisfied that I had everything of importance, I took a deep breath, tossed the backpack over my right shoulder, and launched myself into the night, never to look back in the direction of the life I was abandoning. I wasn't about to stay where I felt unwanted. Part of my mind was saying that I shouldn't run away, that my family did care for me, but those thoughts were overruled by my certainty that I should just leave, walk away. If they truly cared, they wouldn't be arguing over which of them would have to take me into their home.

Thus began my journey with no destination. I was clueless as to where I was headed. I figured I would walk as far away from the West Side, where I had always lived, until I found a different world. I headed east, walking blindly, lost in thought and paying no attention to my surroundings. I felt no fear, for I knew almost everyone in the community. My grandmother Aldine and my Aunt Ruby were well-known. They had opened Operation Life, a non-profit organization that provided free medical aide to those in need, along with a WIC program, a day care center for low income families, and a job training center. I was compelled to assist in its operation from the beginning. I was appointed leader of a program called *Be Like Me, Drug Free*, whose goal was to steer kids away from the temptation to use or sell drugs.

As I walked, I could hear Squeegee hissing from inside my backpack. I could see him looking up at me from deep within the pack, his beady eyes shining like red gemstones. He was pure white, a birthday gift from my grandmother three years earlier, so tiny at only six weeks old. But boy, did he stink! My grandmother finally had the veterinarian remove his scent glands. I think Squeegee was as happy about it as we were, because he was never thrilled with the daily bubble baths and scented shampoos that were our only means of controlling his strong body odor.

Squeegee was easy to train, but, true to his breed, he had a fetish for shiny objects and was expert at hiding things. He kept my grandmother in a constant state of frustration because he always hid away her car keys and jewelry. It reached the point that she blamed Squeegee when it was actually she whom had misplaced an item. I quickly learned that this was just her way of showing her love for the little guy.

I had been walking for hours. I was nowhere near the West Side any longer. My feet ached and I cursed the Jordan sneakers on my feet, having neglected to change into my Oasics running shoe before setting out. I squinted at the black plastic Timex watch on my left wrist, but its numbers were elusive in the darkness, the natural blue indigo had reached its demise months ago. The streetlights offered no assistance. The streets were virtually quiet.

I soon realized that I had walked to a familiar street where my best friend, Big Dee, lived nearby. A few cars sped past me, heading in the opposite direction, introducing gusts of pre-dawn coolness to my skin and face, and sending chills up my spine. I rubbed my arms to calm the goosebumps that had appeared there.

As I continued toward Big Dee's apartment, I heard a growling sound close-by. I paused to observe my surroundings and saw nothing that posed a threat, so I continued along my way. The growling came again, louder than before. I froze and squinted into the shadows around me, searching for the source. When it came once more, I slid the backpack from my shoulder so I could check on Squeegee, worried that he had heard the growl and might be afraid, as I was. I felt foolish when I recognized Squeegee curled into a ball, sound asleep, and snoring loudly. I had never heard him snore with such deep resonance. I reached inside to awaken him, and noticed the bag of ferret snacks was empty.

"Squeege!" He didn't budge, not even when I lightly plucked him on top of the head with my index finger. "See, man, Squeegee, you done ate up all your food and I don't have the money to buy you no more!" He might as well have been in a coma, for he didn't twitch at all at the sound of my agitated voice. I tucked the blue blanket around him snugly to protect him from the cool air, shouldered the backpack and started across the intersection toward Big Dee's apartment complex.

I ambled through a Kentucky Fried Chicken parking lot and into a small empty lot. As I approached the front of the gateless complex, I noticed a group of four well-dressed Hispanics standing around a royal blue Ford

F150 pickup. Two men and two women. They each held bottles of beer. The ladies were dressed in sexy outfits. The low cut tight pants showed their curves and their halter tops displayed their flat stomachs. Both men wore black jeans with huge silver belt buckles and colorful long-sleeved western style button-up shirts, black cowboy boots with silver-tipped toes. One of them wore a snow white cowboy hat. I assumed they had been out partying all night and just didn't want the fun to end quite yet. They noticed me when I appeared out of the darkness of the empty lot. I waved a lazy right hand in their direction as I crossed the street to take a shortcut through the dirt yards in the complex. The man in the white hat gave it a little tip in my direction, acknowledging my greeting.

I strolled across the hard-packed dirt yards with an attentive stride, assuring myself that I would not become victim once again of the nearly invisible clothes lines that were everywhere. I had learned my lesson several years ago, not to be in a hurry to get through these yards in the dark. I had found myself nearly decapitated and flipped onto my back on the hard dirt surface, left breathless and gasping, with a nice welt across my throat where I had run into one of the invisible cables that had been strung. The dim yellow lights from back porches weren't much help, either.

When I arrived at Big Dee's flat and raised my hand to knock on the door, I suddenly paused when I remembered the early hour. It would not be a good idea to upset Dee's mother. I stood there collecting my thoughts, trying to devise a plan to get Dee's attention without waking her mom. I recalled that Dee's bedroom was just to the right of the door, so I eased my way to her window and tapped, loudly whispering her name. When there was no response, I decided she must be camping out in the living room, where I knew she felt more comfortable sleeping.

I was hungry, cold, and exhausted, and my feet were killing me. Now I was wondering if it had been such a great idea to run away, as well. *Silly me*, I tongue lashed myself. Great. Now I was talking to myself. I sighed in frustration and lifted my face to the sky, inhaling a great breath of fresh air in hopes to clear my head, trying to make some sense of my ordeal. I watched the new day begin to dawn, forcing the shadows back and the night away. Just as the sun began to shed its first rays across the land, I decided it was time to go ahead and risk waking Big Dee's mother. I had to get off my feet and get some rest and food! I knew she couldn't stay angry at me for long.

The door vibrated in its frame as I banged my fist. It sounded much louder than the effort I was putting into the task. My surroundings were so quiet and still, it was the only sound for miles, I assumed. I heard movement inside the flat and watched the peephole darken for a moment. Several locks were clicked open and the door opened only as far as the security chain would allow. I could see Big Dee's right eye as she peered through, trying to recognize who could be at her door at this odd hour of the morning.

The door quickly closed and I heard the security chain being released from its post, then the door opened wide. It was Big Dee, my best friend in the whole wide world, who I hadn't seen in weeks. She was Hispanic, very beautiful, with the most gorgeous transformational hazel eyes I had ever seen. Her long jet black hair hung gracefully to the small of her back. She was very curvaceous with a tapered waist and humongous breasts, a real brick house. I estimated she was physically developed and matured ten years in advance of her fourteen years of age. Always quick to take up a motherly or big sisterly stance in my life. I was older than she was, only by one year, but still, I was older and felt I was the one who should be the advisor and protector. And man, I tell you. Big Dee was overly protective of me, so much to the point she insisted that I learn to speak Spanish, and you guessed it, she would be the teacher.

Her reason as to why I needed to learn the language, she said it would come in handy and it would help me be aware of those who might speak negatively about me and/or have ill feelings toward me. I really didn't know what she was getting at. I honestly didn't care about the meaningless opinions of others, but I decided to let her teach me her native language anyway, just to make her happy. Then, when I became fluent in Spanish, she tells me to keep it a secret, not to let others know I spoke the language. This damn girl had her nerve, demanding that I learn a new language and then turn around in the same breath and say keep it a secret, not to speak it. *But what damn sense does that make if I can't use what I learn,* I thought. There was a method to my best friend's madness and it was only obvious that there would be a hidden clause somewhere between her request and reasons, which was, I was only to speak Spanish to her and out the presence of others. I didn't even attempt to contest her request, which was more demand than request. I was going to do whatever I wanted to do regardless, but out of respect and loyalty for her, I would honor her instruction. Big Dee stepped aside out of the doorway to invite me in. She closed the door behind me and secured the locks.

"Where is moms at? Sleep?" I asked in passing heading toward the fridge to get a bite.

She must have been following my actions because she said, "I don't know what you expect to find in there 'cause ain't nothing to eat in there, not even a grunion."

I cracked the fridge door anyway to take inventory of its contents. I grimaced at the two items that shared the spacious icebox. A makeshift water jug made from a plastic gallon milk container sat on the top rack, half full, and a thin but tall glass jar filled with yellowish liquid was cradled on the inner side of the fridge door, its label read yellow chili pepper, but there was not one of the small hot pods immersed in the juice. It was unlike Big Dee and her mother not to have any food in the fridge. I couldn't recall ever seeing it so empty. It had always had at least some sort of lunch meat, TV dinners, or leftovers from last night's evening meal. "Damn!" I mumbled below a whisper.

I assumed Dee must of heard me utter my disappointment or she had came to the conclusion that I was upset from the way I slammed the fridge door closed, because she said sarcastically, "I told you."

I told you my ass! Why ain't no damn food in the spot? What the hell is really goin' on around here? Y'all on a hunger strike or some type of fast or diet? Maaan! 'Cause I told you shit ain't cuttin' it for my stomach, I mentally rambled off.

I turned to check the cabinets for canned goods. I was sure there would be a can of beef stew, or fruit cocktail, refried beans, or at least a jar of peanut butter, if nothing else, collecting dust on a shelf for drastic moments like this?

I pulled open one of the cabinet doors above the counter top. A group of cockroaches must have been eavesdropping and waiting on me to open up the door, because when I did, they dove out as if they were sky diving. They hit the counter top and scattered for cover. The presence of the roaches didn't take me by surprise, not even their action, for I have had numerous run-ins with the brown vermin and witnessed similar performances on more than one occasion at a relative's apartment.

I ambled back into the living room and took up a seat on the small couch where Big Dee was holdin' camp. I removed the backpack from my shoulder and set it on the floor, then shed the Jordans from my aching feet and sank lazily into the rough wool sofa, gazing about the unattractive living room that was familiar. A carpetless

266

floor, one wooden end table against a wall with a mini stereo and one small speaker on its surface. The small couch that Big Dee and I occupied was the only substantial piece of furniture that decorated the room. The couch faced the front door but was positioned in the far back of the room only a few feet away from the huge glass patio door that led to a small porch. Dee had broke the silence between us. "Boo, what time is it about?" she asked sleepily. I didn't bother to answer the question for I had questions of my own.

"What's up with no food in the spot?" I began, "And where is Moms?" I inquired, now staring at Dee's pretty, smooth face, mentally outlining the details that make her so beautiful and unique. She told me she hadn't seen her mother in weeks and that she was worried because mom normally would call to check in and drop off groceries and lunch money for school. I asked Dee if she knows where her mom was resting at? She said she didn't know and mom wasn't giving any information to her whereabouts or how she could be contacted. All she knew was that her mother was with a man who normally accompanied her when she would come home to drop groceries and money. This explained why there was no food in the house; or did it, I wondered?

I quickly became upset with Dee's mom for being so irresponsible and selfish, and for choosing some chump over her own daughter. The high level of respect I previously had for her quickly diminished, 'cause I felt she has placed my homegirl in harm's way by leaving her alone and exposed to the sick predators that prowl the streets. But I was more furious with Big Dee than I was with her mother, 'cause Dee knew she should have called me and let me know she was living alone while her mother ran around with some dude. I knew in my heart Dee was capable of taking care of herself, but that wasn't the point. Dee is legally still a child and her mother's responsibility, and such responsibility was being neglected, as far as I was concerned.

It was Dee's turn to quiz me about what I was doing out and about at that time of the morning. I told her about my grandmother passing away and my relatives arguing about which of them was going to have to take me in, and so I had simply run away from the whole scene. With tears in her eyes, she rose from her end of the couch and pulled me into her arms, giving me a huge bear hug and practically smothering me as she crushed my face into her huge soft breasts.

I hadn't allowed myself to cry over my grandmother's death, but when I felt Big Dee's heart beating against mine and knew that I was finally in the presence of someone who actually cared about me, I lost all composure and cried like a little baby until I couldn't cry no more. Dee shared the tears with me while assuring me that everything would be okay and that she would be there for me, through thick and thin, no matter what. In my heart I knew her words was genuine, for she has always protected me as though I was her newborn child. She was the only person on this earth I would allow to see my sensitive side.

She finally released her bear hug. I sucked in the air as though I had been under water. We sat facing each other. She wiped the tears away from my face then caressed my cheeks with the tips of her fingers. She told me I was always welcome to camp out at the house and demanded that I get comfortable, because I would be staying. I certainly didn't turn down her offer, because I did need a place to lay my head until I figured out my next move.

I heard the growl again, but this time it was my empty stomach. I removed the loose change from my front pocket and slowly counted it several times for accuracy, not wanting to accept the fact that I had only two dollars, sixty-five cents to my name. I figured that I could buy a grab size bag of Dorito's tortilla chips, a king-size Snickers Bar and a Big Gulp soda and share it with Dee. Yeah, that's what I would do, I figured. I asked Dee was she hungry. She shot me a most irritated look in answer to my stupid question.

"Why? You got some money to buy us something to eat?" she asked.

"I have two dollars and sixty-five cents to get us something to take the cheat off us," I replied, holding out the hand with the loose change.

"Boo, that's enough to get us something to eat for a few days!" She was excited.

Yeah? I wondered what in the world we could possibly buy with two dollars and sixty-five cents to last us for two days. If Dee said we could, then we could. She knew better than I did. I figured that I'd just follow her lead because she was the expert shopper. We decided to stroll to the store, but first I headed to her restroom for a quick pit stop. I was stopped in my tracks when I heard Big Dee screaming in fear.

I ran back into the living room to see what was wrong. I found Dee standing on the arm of the sofa, her eyes as big as dinner plates. At first, I noticed nothing that posed a threat. "Girl, what the hell wrong with you?" My heart was pounding hard from being taken by surprise. She pointed to the floor. I looked down and had to laugh when I saw Squeegee, who had freed himself from the backpack and was attempting to make friends with Dee. He was sitting up on his rump and waving his little arms in the air. Dee had never met him, and her reaction was perfectly normal, because ferrets are often mistaken for large rats.

I ambled over and lifted him into my arms, tickling his tummy. It took Dee several minutes to calm down before she attempted to get acquainted with Squeegee. I left the two of them alone while I finally hit the john, then the three of us headed out to the grocery store on foot. I wasn't happy about the fact that I had to put my shoes back on, so I tucked the laces inside and slipped into them, which was much more comfortable. I shouldered the backpack with Squeegee inside and we all headed out to our destination.

CHAPTER 2

The glass doors opened as we approached the front of the store. I followed Big Dee down one of the long aisles. She was obviously familiar with the store's layout, because she knew exactly where to find the items she wanted. She removed twelve packages of Top Ramen noodles from a lower shelf, handed them to me, then ambled into the refrigerated section. She snagged a package of 99-cent chicken hot dogs, and then headed toward the produce section.

We stopped at eight huge wooden barrels that were filled with assorted candies. Each barrel had a clear Plexiglas lid. Big Dee began sampling the sweet treats as quickly as possible. I quickly followed her lead, plunging one hand in a barrel of gummy bears while my other hand was removing a half dozen sweet and sour gummy worms from the next barrel. I made my way down to the last barrel, which hosted my favorite candy inside, chocolate covered raisins. I scooped up a handful and stuffed my mouth as I followed Dee out of the aisle. We went to the quick checkout line, twelve items or less, which had a pretty long line of customers waiting to pay for their purchases. I ambled over to a candy and magazine rack. I removed the backpack from my shoulder and set it on the floor in front of me, then snagged the *King* magazine from the rack and swiftly flipped through its pages to peep the centerfold honeys, then snatched up a copy of *Coup D'etat Illustrated* and began skimming through it, too.

In a couple of minutes, Big Dee could be heard calling me to come pay for our items. I replaced the mag, shouldered my pack and quickly returned to the cash register and paid for the items. A total of two dollars seventeen cents for twelve Top Ramen and a pack of hot dogs. *Not bad for a couple of bucks,* I thought. We headed back to Big Dee's flat.

The sun was shining down full blast by then, and I was exhausted. I took up my original spot on the couch while Big Dee did her thang in the kitchen. I had just dozed off when she tapped my shoulder and handed me the bowel of grub she prepared. I didn't even growl about being awakened, which would have been my normal reaction. I must have been starvin' for I practically inhaled the food. I never realized just how good a soup with chopped up hot dogs would be. I guess anything is good when you're hungry. We ate hot dogs and Top Ramen for the next two days, just like she said we could. Even Squeegee nibbled on Bid Dee's concocted delicacy. But our food supply quickly dwindled. *Dee's mom need to bring her ass home and drop off some ends,* I thought.

I took up camp in Dee's room while Squeegee hung out with Dee on the couch. I was pretty depressed as well as grieving for my granny, so I stayed isolated in Dee's bedroom sleeping as long as I could until Dee felt the need for more company other than Squeegee.

I was awakened from a deep sleep by a bad dream I was having. I rose onto my elbows, held my face in my hands and debated whether I wanted to get up, still feeling a little sluggish. Coming from the living room, I heard the faint sound of music, laughter, and Dee's voice demanding someone stop doing something. I waited for a few seconds to try and make out what Dee was saying. I figured that Squeegee was giving her a hard time because she probably hadn't given him any attention. I laid back down until I heard Dee's voice rise a few decibels. I jumped up to go see what was going on. I entered the living room unnoticed.

Dee had a house full of company. Three of her female friends, scantily clad and with far too much makeup on, and two Hispanic adult males who were clearly members of the southerner Mexican gang, the tattoos on their arms and neck confirming their gang affiliation. One of the thugs was rough handling Squeegee, slapping him around aggressively as though he was training a pit bull to fight. Squeegee growled and fought back to the best of his ability but he was no match for the bully. I damn near lost my mind when I seen my little Squeegee being treated so crude. I was beyond furious and quickly took his place. "Man, what's your --

" I swiftly darted in for the kill with a cruel overhand that found its target.

The dude squealed a painful groan when my fist introduced itself to his chin. He fell backwards to the floor before my left hook could do any damage. He was out cold. Squeegee ran up my leg and into my arms, breathing heavily, happy to see me.

"Nooo! Joker, that's my best friend!" Big Dee shouted, running over and stepping between us. The gang banger she called Joker had pulled out a gun. I frowned at him and tried to shove Dee out the line of fire with my right hand, but she didn't budge.

"Say Ese! You done fucked up by putting your hands on my boy, homes," Joker said waving the gun. "Ese, get out my way so I can smoke this fool," Joker ordered Big Dee.

She wouldn't budge. Joker attempted to move around her but she kept blocking him, pleading and explaining that I am her best friend, the one she had told him about and she was not going to allow him to shoot me. Joker demanded that I give his unconscious friend a fair fight. Big Dee accepted on my behalf as long as he promised not to involve any guns. Joker tucked his gun away. I took that as he accepted Dee's proposal.

"Flako! Get your ass up, Ese!" Joker tugged at his friend's arm. "Get your ass up and represent the three SUR gang!" Joker growled.

Flako was just coming to, still dazed. He managed to get to his feet with the help of Joker. "I'm gonna kill you, Ese," Flako threatened and took a fighting stance.

"Hold down, Ese," Joker said placing an open hand on Flako's chest, then gazed in my direction and continued. "Let's take this outside."

No problem fool! Let's go outside. Outside, inside, it doesn't matter where we do the damn thing at, it's all the same to me, you got to bring a ass to get some ass, I mentally expressed.

"Aight, let's handle that, then," I said, placing Squeegee on the floor.

"I got your back, Boo," Big Dee whispered into my ear.

I knew she did, no doubt about it. Big Dee was my best friend, my sister by another father and mother, and my mother of another lifetime. Of course she had by back unconditionally, a fact I've been absolutely sure of for several years now. I made my way outside. I knew if anything was to go down foul, Dee was able to hold her own, because I taught her good how to scrap and she was a beast when it came to chunking 'em. If I had to choose any one of my friends to catch my back, it would most definitely be Dee.

I stepped out the door and was dope fiend by Flako and sent sprawling in the dirt front yard. I tried by best to regain my balance, but the unexpected blow to the head had dazed me to the point that my equilibrium wasn't able to recoup fast enough before I hit the ground. I lay there on the cold hard pack dirt yard trying to compose myself.

"Now, that's what I'm talkin' about, Ese. That's how a true SUR do it," Joker cheered.

"Boo, get up and whup that fool," Big Dee cried out. "You know that's fucked up of you Flako to dope fiend him like that. What! You afraid that you would get your ass kicked on a head up fade? That's why you had to blindside him. Huh?"

"Bitch, you watch your mouth and shut the hell up before I do your ass the same way," Flako snapped back.

Big Dee squared up with Flako, "Well, what's wrong with your doin'? Brang it!" She challenged. By that time I had stumbled to my feet and found my footing.

"Dee! Dee! Get out the way and let me handle my business," I grunted. She stepped to the side to let me face my opponent.

Flako laughed and smiled cunningly and said, "You still want more, Ese?"

"I got a dub on my homie Flako. Which one of you want to bet?" Joker asked looking in the direction of the three girls who was watching the action.

"I'll bet you," Big Dee announced. "I got a twenty spot on my boy Boo, that he stump a mud hole in Flako ass," she said.

"Bet!" Joker accepted. "And I want my money right after your little boyfriend get knocked out."

I wondered what Dee thought she was doing, betting on her brown ass, because she didn't have money, not one dime to her name. If I lose, then what? Then there's really gonna be some shit. Joker gonna flip and most likely bust a cap in both of our asses. That was an issue I couldn't be worrying myself with at the moment because it didn't exist, for I hadn't lost yet, and hadn't no intentions on losing.

Flako made his move. A crisp left jab caught me on the bridge of the nose that left me teary eyed, followed by a deafening right hook to the ear. I howled in pain. Seeing that I was in distress, Flako rushed in for the kill with a powerful leaping left hook. I tucked my chin and turned my right shoulder into the punch in the nick of time to give the blow a durable target. I countered with a straight right to the chest that backed him up a few steps. Dee cheered me on from the sideline. Flako was no punk. It was obvious that he had some training in boxing because he held his hands up high, chin tucked, and he knew how to put his body weight behind his punches. The only flaw that I noticed was that he was a headhunter, a real big mistake when it came to fighting an experienced fighter. He delivered a well placed kidney shot that nearly folded me. I realized then, I could no longer underestimate Flako, and if I was to beat him I would have to step up my A-game, which I did.

I slipped a left jab, then a straight right and pivoted out to his right side, releasing a four-piece combo, then dipped out to the left and fired a twelve-piece flurry of jabs, upper cuts and hooks to the head and body which folded him like a lounge chair. Flako was down for the count.

Big Dee jumped in excitement shouting, "That's my homeboy, my boy. I told you my homeboy was gonna kick his ass. Let me get paid, break mine off!" She held out her hand toward Joker.

He slapped it away and growled coldly, "Bitch, I'm not givin' you shit, not one red dime. So you might as well chalk that up as a loss and get out of my face."

"What!" Big Dee was pissed off now. I knew that Dee was not going to accept that. She had a very serious problem with someone taking something from her, and Joker had refused to give up something that she felt entitled to.

"Oh, you gonna pay me or get your ass whup'd out here real proper like," she said pointing her finger in his face.

He shoved her aggressively, the wrong thing to do in front of me. She threw two haymakers at his chin that hit nothing but air. I launched in to take her place with a right body shot that followed a gruesome left upper cut that put Joker on his back. He swiftly leapt back to his feet. I got ready to deliver another attack, one more grisly than the first, but found myself staring down the barrel of a gun. Joker wiped at his bloody mouth with the back of his left hand, keeping aim with the other. He spat a wad of the bright red fluid, glanced up with his eyes full of hatred and growled, "Bitch, how about tryin' that Mike Tyson shit now and see if you can stand up under the seventeen blows I'm gonna hit yo' ass with." Then smiled a ghostly one, stepping forward.

Dee pleaded for my life, but her words fell on deaf ears. I knew I was a dead man, so I took what might be my last chance for survival. I could only hope my martial arts training and speed would pay off. I swiftly pivoted, grasped his wrist, turning my back in toward his chest. I snapped my elbow back into his face, pivoted back out, twisted the hand that gripped the gun and bending him over backwards. I snapped a consecutive flying knee to his jaw that knocked him unconscious.

I removed the gun from his hand and tucked it in my waistband, then searched his pockets and came up on a small wad. I shuffled through the bills. "Thirteen funky ass dollas," I grunted. "Dee, this, chump only had thirteen lousy ass dollas," I said and handed her the singles.

"What!" She frowned and recounted the bread. Joker hadn't the money to cover the debt from the beginning, just as Dee hadn't, but does that make them even? No! I thought. Regardless, right or wrong, that thirteen bucks belonged to Dee, and we were going keep it because I had to knock the chump out for disrespecting my homegirl. Plus, we needed the money badly. I knew she would accept the thirteen bucks and be cool with it, considering the circumstances. There was nothing she could do about it anyway, right? Joker didn't have more money or anything else of value on his person. It's only common sense that you can't squeeze water out of a dry rag.

Dee's girlfriends had split after the action was over. No good byes, no I'll see you laters, no I'll holla at cha's, no nothing, just a magician's trick, vanishing in the air, the three girls had broke wide into the wind. Dee and I strolled back inside the flat, leaving our adversaries laid out in the yard.

I secured the locks on the door, washed my hands, then retrieved Squeegee to give him a thorough examination to be sure he had not suffered any broken bones or serious injuries. Once I was satisfied that Squeegee was okay, I removed the weapon I had taken off Joker, dropped the clip from its sleeve and jacked the slide to extract the loaded round from its chamber. A nice piece of metal, I thought. Just what I needed in case Joker and Flako returned with a slew of their gang member buddies to retaliate. I assured myself I wouldn't hesitate to use it to protect myself, Dee, and Squeegee.

Dee must have had a similar fear of them returning, for she flopped down next to me and rested her head against my shoulder while clutching tightly to the handle of a huge butcher knife. I'd never seen such a cruel design. Just the look of it frightened me, but I knew that knife would be no good if Joker and his crew was to return, because they would most definitely be packing guns. Dee and I sat in silence as she watched me reload the weapon.

Squeegee had made himself comfortable on my lap. Several hours passed. I assumed that was a sign that Joker and Flako would not be showing up for revenge, so I broke the silence between Dee and I. We chatted for a long while and decided that we would sell the gun. She knew of a fence who would take if off our hands. Although I didn't want to let it go, we needed the bread for immediate necessities. I had planned to head out in the morning to the union hall for a job, and union dues would hit me for forty bucks that I didn't have. Dee

80

made the call to her fence. He swooped through and offered eighty bucks for the piece. I nodded to Dee and she accepted the offer. She slid me two dubs for union dues and held onto the other half for groceries.

Squeegee wouldn't let me out of his sight. Everywhere I went, he stayed on my heels. He made it clear that he wouldn't be doing no more camping out in the living room with Dee when he dragged his blanket into the bedroom where I was holding camp. I grabbed the backpack to get his water bottle. To my surprise, it was crammed with candy bars, bubble gum, and a grab bag of open Lay's potato chips.

"What the hell?" Then I realized where the goodies came from and how they'd gotten in the bag. I thought back to the store at the candy and magazine rack were I was thumbing through the magazines. I recalled sitting the backpack on the floor in front of me. "That little thief," I said to no one other than myself with a smirk on my face as I eyeballed the goods. There was no doubt in my mind who the shoplifter was. Who else was so attracted to shimmering and colorful objects? Who else had a long track record and tendency of tiptoeing away with property that didn't belong to them? Who else was so cute and innocent looking? Who most likely would never be suspected or thought of having the capability of committing a crime? Squeegee, of course, my little white furry pet ferret friend.

I called to Dee and she came rushing into the room with a worried expression plastered on her face. "What's up?" She huffed, heart pounding against her chest like a bass drum as her right hand clenched tightly around the handle of the butcher knife. I played it off like I didn't notice her paranoid behavior.

"Come an' get you some of this candy and chips, compliments of Squeegee," I said with a smile. She moved over to the bed and picked out the items she desired. I couldn't help but eye the knife. Just the sight of it sent chills up my spine. "Girl, won't you put that Friday the thirteen lookin' ass machete up somewhere before you hurt yourself?" I teased.

She shot me a devilish smirk before turning toward the door and said, "Good night Boo. Go on and get you some rest if you plan to go job huntin' in the morning." She flicked down the light switch and closed the door behind her.

"I love you too, girl," I whispered.

-- o0o --

ABOUT THE AUTHORS

Timothy R. Richardson, aka *TipToe*, is a multi-talented producer and Hip Hop artist and founder of Crime Wave Clothing. He is also co-author of The *Other Side of the Mirror, Head Gamez,* and *Players Exposed.* He is from Oakland, California.

Eugene L. Weems is the bestselling author of *United We Stand* and award winning author of *Prison Secrets.* Weems is co-author of *The Other Side of the Mirror, Head Gamez, and Players Exposed* and *Bound by Loyalty.*

The former kick boxing champion is a producer, model, philanthropist, and founder of No Question Apparel and Inked Out Beef books. He is from Las Vegas, Nevada.

Head Gamez

Eugene L. Weems
Timothy R. Richardson

When a team of four beautiful but deadly assassins are given covert assignments to track down and eliminate Hip Hop's biggest Gangsta Rappers….

"Who gets hit next in this crazy game of killers for hire?"

The world may never find the right man, because sometimes the best man for the job is a woman.

14.95   325 pgs   6x9 Paperback   ISBN: 978-0-9840456-1-7

UNITED WE STAND

A TRIBUTE TO THE AMERICAN FALLEN HEROES OF THE WAR ON TERRORISM

By Eugene L. Weems

United We Stand is a beautiful collection of inspirational artwork and passion-filled poetry created as a living tribute to the American troops who have made the ultimate sacrifice for our country in the war against terrorism.

100% of the proceeds from this book will be contributed to provide care packages for the active duty troops who remain engaged in the war overseas and provide college scholarship trust funds for the children of our American fallen heroes.

$14.95   95 pgs   6x9 Paperback   ISBN: 978-1-4251-9130-6

Hip Hop/Music

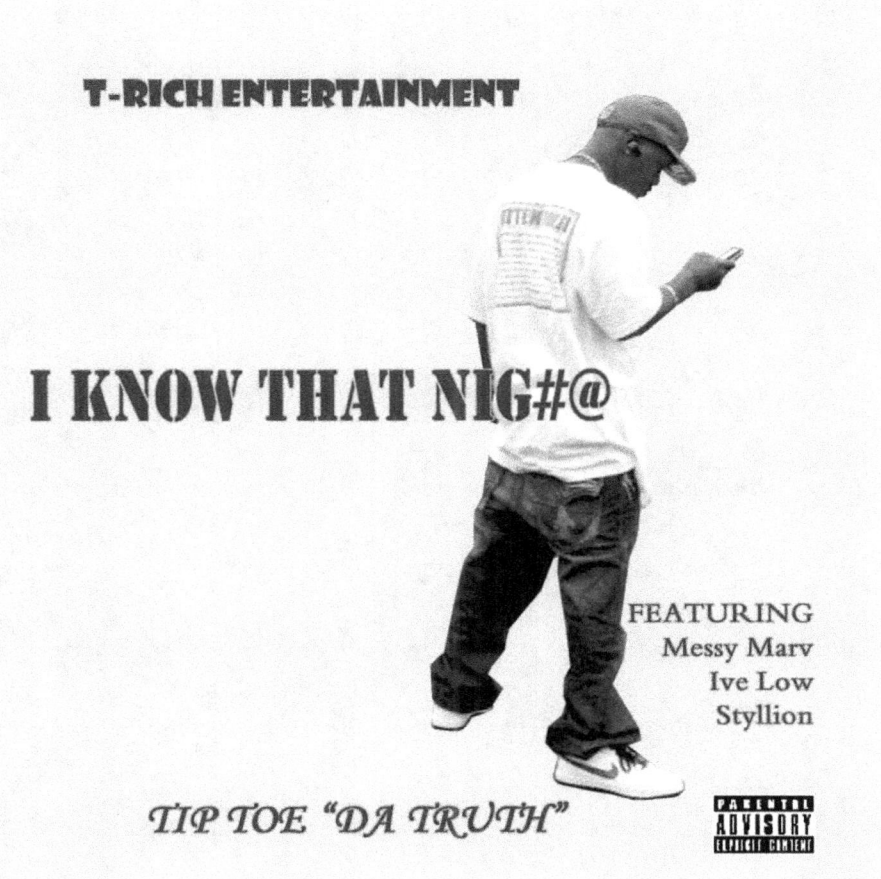

WWW.UNIVERSALPUBLISHINGLLC.COM

Available Now

JACKSON RANCH RESCUE Feline Sanctuary is a nonprofit organization which aids abused, abandoned, injured and neglected felines.

We rescue animals in distress whenever an urgent call is received. Our volunteers work with feral cats to help them become familiar with humans so they can be adopted. We have had much success in this area.

Your generous support and assistance is needed. You can help by making a charitable contribution that will go toward the food, shelter and veterinary care, including spay and neuter costs, for these beautiful animals. Your contribution is tax deductible and will be gratefully received.

Contributions can be sent through PayPal using our email address: jacksonranchrescue@juno.com.

THANK YOU FOR YOUR GENEROSITY

www.ingramcontent.com/pod-product-compliance
Lightning Source LLC
Chambersburg PA
CBHW070305260626
47160CB00003B/730